Nathan Smith Davis

Contributions to the history of medical education and medical institutions in the United States of America. 1776-1876. Special report

Antigonos

Nathan Smith Davis

Contributions to the history of medical education and medical institutions in the United States of America. 1776-1876. Special report

Reprint of the original, first published in 1877.

1st Edition 2024 | ISBN: 978-3-38612-132-3

Antigonos Verlag is an imprint of Outlook Verlagsgesellschaft mbH.

Verlag (Publisher): Outlook Verlag GmbH, Zeilweg 44, 60439 Frankfurt, Deutschland, info@outlook-verlag.de
Vertretungsberechtigt (Authorized to represent): E. Roepke, Zeilweg 44, 60439 Frankfurt, Deutschland
Druck (Print): Libri Plureos GmbH, Friedensallee 273, 22763 Hamburg, Deutschland

CONTRIBUTIONS TO THE HISTORY

OF

MEDICAL EDUCATION AND MEDICAL INSTITUTIONS

IN THE

UNITED STATES OF AMERICA.

1776—1876.

SPECIAL REPORT.

PREPARED FOR THE

UNITED STATES BUREAU OF EDUCATION

BY

N. S. DAVIS, A. M., M. D.

WASHINGTON:
GOVERNMENT PRINTING OFFICE.
1877.

CONTENTS.

II.—SOCIAL MEDICAL ORGANIZATIONS.

LETTER.

————

DEPARTMENT OF THE INTERIOR,
BUREAU OF EDUCATION,
Washington, D. C., October 13, 1877.

SIR: The plan of preparation for the Centennial Exhibition undertaken by this Bureau embraced a special report on the progress of medical education during the century. J. M. Toner, M. D., of this city, had furnished a valuable contribution to the history of medical education prior to the Revolution, which was published by the Bureau in 1874. After consultation with him and others a request to prepare the medical portion of the educational history for the century was addressed to N. S. Davis, A. M., M. D., of Chicago, as one eminently fitted to perform such a task successfully and to the satisfaction of the medical profession. Dr. Davis cheerfully undertook the work, for which his previous labors, educational and historical, specially qualified him.

The report on public libraries was the first portion published of the historical series intended to bring the progress of education in the United States down to the Centennial year. Dr. Davis's work on medical education is the second subject ready for the printer.

There are many indications of the increase of public and professional interest in advancing the standard of medical education, and it is believed that Dr. Davis's monograph will be a valuable contribution to this end, while it will afford this Office the means of replying to many inquiries addressed to it on the subject.

I have the honor hereby to recommend its immediate publication.

Very respectfully, your obedient servant,

JOHN EATON,
Commissioner.

The Hon. SECRETARY OF THE INTERIOR.

Approved, and publication ordered.

C. SCHURZ,
Secretary.

PREFACE.

Soon after commencing the work of compiling the following history an invitation was received to deliver an address, on the progress of medical education in the United States during the past century, before the International Medical Congress, which had been called to assemble in Philadelphia in September, 1876. In performing that duty, the same facts and in some instances the same language were used as in the following pages. In 1850, the writer published a small volume, entitled "History of medical education and institutions in the United States, from the first settlement of the British colonies to the year 1850." Only one edition was printed, and that has been entirely out of the market for more than fifteen years. I have, therefore, copied freely from such parts of it as would aid me in preparing the present work, without using quotation marks, or always making marginal references.

N. S. DAVIS.

MEDICAL EDUCATION AND MEDICAL INSTITUTIONS.

INTRODUCTION.

The medical profession in this and every other civilized country is so closely connected with the social and sanitary condition of the people on the one hand, and with the status of education and general science on the other, that its progress in the past and its position in the present are deserving of the most careful attention. This is preëminently true concerning the profession in this country, whose institutions have all had their origin since the beginning of the seventeenth century and their development in the midst of an educated and free people.

The history of the medical profession and its institutions during the colonial period, extending from the first settlement of the country by Europeans to the Declaration of Independence in 1776, has been so fully developed in the work of Dr. James Thacher, entitled "American Medical Biography," published in two volumes, in 1828, in which he gave what he calls "A succinct history of medical science in the United States from the first settlement of the country;" in the paper entitled "History of American Medicine before the Revolution," by John B. Beck, M. D.;* in the first chapter of a volume entitled "History of Medical Education and Institutions in the United States," &c.,† and more recently in a monograph published under the direction of the Bureau of Education, written by J. M. Toner, M. D.,‡ that I need not include that period in my present work. From the date of the first English settlement in 1607, to the Declaration of Independence in 1776, thirteen separate colonies had been established, embracing the Atlantic coast from Massachusetts to Georgia, inclusive, and all acknowledging allegiance to the government of Great Britain. Distributed over this wide extent of territory there had accumulated about three million people, among whom there were between three thousand and thirty-five hundred engaged in the practice of medicine. Of these, it has been estimated that not more than four hundred had received the degree of M. D. from a medical college,§ and most of these had received their collegiate education and honors in Europe. Only two medical colleges had been organized in the colonies, viz, the Medical College of Philadelphia, now

---

* See Transactions of the Medical Society of the State of New York.

† See History of Medical Education, by N. S. Davis, M. D., Chicago, 1851.

‡ See Contributions to the Annals of Medical Progress and Medical Education in the United States, before and during the War of Independence, by J. M. Toner, M. D., 1874.

§ Ibid., page 106.

the medical department of the University of Pennsylvania, in 1765; and the medical department of King's (now Columbia) College, in New York, in 1768. But only fifty-one medical degrees had been conferred by both these institutions prior to the year 1776, when active operations were suspended by the progress of the war. In all the colonies there were not more than twelve or fifteen cities and towns having over five thousand inhabitants, and these were so widely separated from each other, with such limited means for communication, that the attendance on a medical college or on the meetings of medical societies was surrounded with delays and difficulties but little thought of at the present day. The same condition of the country often compelled those practising in the smaller and more remote settlements to combine other occupations with their practice. In the New England colonies the offices of physician and clergyman were often united in the same person, and in all the colonies it was common for the physician to occupy a part of his time and increase his income by engaging to some extent in agriculture. Notwithstanding all the obstacles presented by the sparseness of the population, want of roads, and means of communication, there was an ambition on the part of the physicians to attend at least one course of medical college instruction, and a large proportion had served a regular apprenticeship with some practitioner of note before entering upon the active duties of the profession. Only three medical societies are known to have been organized during the colonial period of our history. The most important of these was the State Medical Society of New Jersey, which was organized in July, 1766. It appears that a few months previous to this a society called the Philadelphia Medical Society was formed in that city, chiefly through the influence of Dr. John Morgan, who had returned from Europe in 1765. It did not probably survive the war for independence, and is not known to have left any permanent record of its doings. The Delaware State Medical Society was organized in 1776.

In nearly all the colonies laws had been enacted concerning topics of interest to the profession. Most of these laws were designed either to protect the people of the colonies from the introduction and spread of contagious diseases, from injury by ignorant and reckless midwives, from exorbitant charges by physicians, or for the establishment of hospitals for the sick and insane. In only two of the colonies were laws enacted to define the qualifications of physicians and surgeons, with provisions for enforcing an observance of the same. The general assembly of New York, in 1760, ordained that "no person whatsoever should practise as physician or surgeon in the city of New York before he shall have been examined in physic and surgery, and approved of and admitted by one of His Majesty's counsel, the judges of the supreme court, the King's attorney general, and the mayor of the city of New York, for the time being, or by any three or more of them, taking to their assistance for such examination such proper person or persons as they in their discretion shall see fit." Such candidates as were approved, received certificates conferring the right to practise physic or surgery, or both, throughout the whole province, and a penalty of £5 was prescribed for all violations of this law.* A similar act was passed by the general assembly of New Jersey in 1772.† Although most of the colonies had provided temporary hospitals for seamen, immigrants, the victims of small pox and other epidemic diseases, the first permanent general hospital for the sick was established in Philadelphia in 1752. It was aided by a grant of £2,000 from the colonial assembly of Pennsylvania; a further grant of £3,000 was made by the provincial assembly in 1762. The building was so far completed in December, 1756, that patients were admitted.‡ Dr. Thomas Bond was appointed superintendent, with Drs. Lloyd Zachary, Thomas Cadwallader, Samuel Preston Moore, John Redman, and Phineas Bond as associates. Dr. Thomas Bond, from the opening of the institution, introduced his class of students for bedside instruction, and thereby became the first regular clinical lecturer in America. A lecture introductory to his clinical course, delivered November, 1766, informs the reader that a copy of it has been placed upon the minute-book of the hospital. The Pennsylvania Hospital Library was begun in 1763, and was for a century the most important collection in the country.

In 1767 the colonial government of New York was induced to grant a charter for a general hospital, and an organization was effected and the work commenced by the laying of the corner-stone in 1773. But the building, when nearly completed, was destroyed by fire in 1775, and owing to the outbreak of the revolutionary war it was not rebuilt until 1791.

From this very brief glance at the condition of medical matters in the colonies, it will be seen that at the commencement of our history as an independent nation, in 1776, there were three or four thousand practitioners supplying three million people, distributed over thirteen States, extending along the Atlantic coast from Massachusetts to Florida, and containing two medical colleges, two organized medical societies, and one permanent general hospital. In noting the progress of the profession during the century which has intervened since that date, we shall arrange the work under the following heads, namely, educational institutions, including colleges and hospitals, and social or society organizations.

I.—MEDICAL COLLEGES AND HOSPITALS.

The credit of delivering the first public lectures on anatomy to a class of medical students in this country, illustrating them by dissections of the

---

*See History of Medical Education and Institutions in the United States, by N. S. Davie, M. D., page 22.

†For interesting details concerning the more prominent members of the profession, laws, customs, &c., in the colonies, the reader is referred to the Annals of Medical Progress, by J. M. Toner, M. D., Washington, 1874.

‡ G. B. Wood's Centennial Address, 1851.

human body, has been awarded Dr. William Hunter, of Newport, R. I., who gave instruction to classes in anatomy from 1752 to 1755. He was a native of Scotland and a relative of the celebrated John and William Hunter, of London. It is quite certain, however, that Dr. Thomas Cadwallader commenced the practice of his profession in Philadelphia as early as 1745, and was engaged in giving instruction to students in anatomy between that period and 1751. But whether his teaching was accompanied by dissections of the human cadaver does not appear. Drs. John Bard and Peter Middleton also dissected the human body for purposes of medical instruction, in New York City, in 1750. Dr. William Shippen, jr., who had recently returned from a protracted period of study in the medical schools and hospitals of London and Edinburgh, commenced a course of anatomical lectures at his father's residence in Philadelphia, in 1762, which was attended by a class of twelve pupils. The lectures were illustrated by actual dissections, the fee for the course being 5 pistoles.* For seeing the subject prepared for the lectures, and learning the art of dissecting, injections, &c., 5 additional pistoles were charged. He also had the use of a series of anatomical plates and casts, donated by Dr. John Fothergill, of London, to the Pennsylvania Hospital.† Dr. Shippen continued his courses of anatomical lectures annually until the organization of the medical department of the Philadelphia College in 1765. During his last two years in Europe he was joined by Dr. John Morgan, who had been educated in Philadelphia and had served one or two years as surgeon in the provincial army, who resigned his position in the army and sailed for London in 1760. Both these gentlemen became favorite pupils of the Hunters in London and took their degrees in medicine at the University of Edinburgh; Dr. Shippen in 1761, and Dr. Morgan in 1763. It was while they were together in London that they appear to have formed a decided purpose to bring about on their return home the establishment of a permanent medical college in Philadelphia. This purpose was not only clearly shown by expressions in their correspondence with friends while in Europe, but was still more plainly indicated in Dr. Shippen's introduction to his first course of lectures, on anatomy in 1762. They not only took special pains to qualify themselves for success in teaching, but they evidently received encouragement from some of the more eminent members of the profession in London and Edinburgh. Thus Dr John Fothergill, when he sent a valuable series of anatomical plates and casts as a gift to the Pennsylvania Hospital, wrote to James Pemberton, in April, 1762, as follows: "In the want of real subjects these will have their use, and I have recommended it to Dr. Shippen to give a course of anatomical lectures to such as may attend. He is very well qualified for the subject, and will soon be followed by an able assistant, Dr. Morgan, both of whom, I apprehend, will not only be useful to

---

* The Spanish pistole is at present worth about four dollars; it was formerly somewhat more valuable.

† See History of Medical Department of the University of Pennsylvania, by Joseph Carson, M. D., pages 42, 43.

the province in their employment, but if suitably countenanced by the legislature will be able to erect a *school of physic* amongst you that may draw students from various parts of America and the West Indies," &c.* It is known that the plans formed by Dr. Morgan in reference to the establishment of a medical college in America were also recommended by Drs. Hunter, Watson, and Cullen. Hon. Thomas Penn, of London, who was a liberal patron of the College of Philadelphia, wrote a letter to the board of trustees of that institution, dated London, February 15, 1765, not only recommending Dr. Morgan, but also advising the establishment of the proposed medical school as a department of that college. †

ESTABLISHMENT OF THE MEDICAL COLLEGE OF PHILADELPHIA.

The College of Philadelphia had been founded in 1749, and received a charter from the proprietaries of the colony, Thomas and Richard Penn, in 1753. Its management was entrusted, in 1765, to a board of trustees twenty-four in number, embracing several of the most eminent citizens, five of whom were physicians, namely, Thomas Bond, Phineas Bond, Thomas Cadwallader, William Shippen, sr., and John Redman. As might have been expected, the board of trustees thus composed gave ready attention to the proposition concerning the establishment of a medical school, and at a meeting held May 3, 1765, Dr. Morgan was unanimously elected "professor of the theory and practice of physic;" thus creating the first medical professorship in America.‡ At a special meeting of the same board of trustees, held September 23, 1765, Dr. William Shippen, jr., was unanimously elected professor of anatomy and surgery. This action of the board of trustees was immediately followed by an official announcement published in the Pennsylvania Gazette of September 26, 1765, as follows :

As the necessity of cultivating medical knowledge in America is allowed by all, it is with pleasure we inform the public that a course of lectures on two of the most important branches of that useful science, viz, anatomy and materia medica, will be delivered this winter in Philadelphia. We have great reason, therefore, to hope that gentlemen of the faculty will encourage the design by recommending it to their pupils, that pupils will themselves be glad of such an opportunity of improvement, and that the public will think it an object worthy of their attention and patronage.

In order to render these courses the more extensively useful, we intend to introduce into them as much of the theory and practice of physic, of pharmacy, chemistry, and surgery as can be conveniently admitted.

From all this, together with an attendance on the practice of the physicians and surgeons of the Pennsylvania Hospital, the students will be able to prosecute their studies with such advantage as will qualify them to practise hereafter with more satisfaction to themselves and benefit to the community.

The particular advertisements inserted below specify the time when these lectures

---

* History of Medical Department of Pennsylvania University, by Joseph Carson, M. D., p. 42.

† Ibid., p. 50.

‡ History of the College of Philadelphia and of the University of Pennsylvania, by Dr. George B. Wood, in vol. iii, Memoirs of Historical Society of Pennsylvania.

are to commence, and contain the various subjects to be treated of in each course, and the terms on which pupils are to be admitted.

WILLIAM SHIPPEN, Jr., M. D.,
Professor of Anatomy and Surgery in the College of Philadelphia.
JOHN MORGAN, M. D., F. R. S., &c.,
Professor of Medicine in the College of Philadelphia.

Although only two professors were appointed, their lectures were made to include most of the branches then regarded as essential to qualify a student to practise the healing art; this preparation was greatly assisted by the clinical teaching of Dr. Thomas Bond in the Pennsylvania Hospital. The arrangement continued a little more than two years, during which time the instruction in the several branches of medicine became more systematic, and the trustees of the college, at a meeting held July 27, 1767, adopted definite rules in regard to the conferring of medical degrees, as follows:*

FOR A BACHELOR'S DEGREE IN PHYSIC.

1. It is required that such students as have not taken a degree in any college shall, before admission to a degree in physic, satisfy the trustees and professors of the college concerning their knowledge in the Latin tongue, and in such branches of mathematics and natural and experimental philosophy as shall be judged requisite to a medical education.

2. Each student shall attend at least one course of lectures in anatomy, materia medica, chemistry, the theory and practice of physic, and one course of clinical lectures, and shall attend the practice of the Pennsylvania Hospital for one year, and may then be admitted to a public examination for a bachelor's degree, provided that, on previous examination by the medical trustees and professors, and such other trustees and professors as choose to attend, such student shall be judged fit to undergo a public examination without attending any more courses in the medical school.

3. It is further required that each student, previous to the bachelor's degree, shall have served a sufficient apprenticeship to some reputable practitioner in physic, and be able to make it appear that he has a general knowledge in pharmacy.

FOR A DOCTOR'S DEGREE IN PHYSIC.

It is required for this degree that at least three years have intervened from the time of taking the bachelor's degree, and that the candidate be full twenty-four years of age, and that he shall write and defend a thesis publicly in the college, unless he should be beyond seas, or so remote on the continent of America as not to be able to attend without manifest inconvenience; in which case, on sending a written thesis, such as shall be approved of by the college, the candidate may receive the doctor's degree ; but his thesis shall be printed and published at his own expense.

This scheme of a medical education is proposed to be on as extensive and liberal a plan as in the most respectable European seminaries ; and the utmost provision is made for rendering a degree a real mark of honor, the reward only of distinguished learning and abilities.

In January, 1768, Dr. Adam Kuhn was elected professor of materia medica and botany ; and the following year Dr. Benjamin Rush was appointed to the chair of chemistry.

---

* See History of Medical Department of University of Pennsylvania, by Joseph Carson, M. D., p. 60.

These appointments, together with the previous adoption of the foregoing regulations concerning qualifications for the degrees of bachelor
and doctor of physic, may be considered as completing the organization
of this important school of medicine.

The announcement of the college session of 1769-'70 promised full
courses of instruction in all the then recognized branches of medical
science, and a session of six months' duration. The faculty stood as follows:

John Morgan, M. D., professor of the theory and practice of medicine.

William Shippen, jr., M. D., professor of anatomy, surgery, and midwifery.

Adam Kuhn, M. D., professor of materia medica and botany.

Benjamin Rush, M. D., professor of chemistry.

Thomas Bond, M. D., professor of clinical medicine.

All these except the last named were young men who had recently
taken their degrees at the University of Edinburgh. While abroad,
they had taken special pains to qualify themselves for teaching in their
respective departments, and it is quite evident that their alma mater
was the model after which they were endeavoring to fashion the new
medical college.

The first medical degree conferred in America was that of bachelor of
medicine. This degree was conferred on ten young men by the Philadelphia College at the public commencement, June 21, 1768. At the commencement June 30th, 1769, the same degree was conferred on eight
students. The degree of doctor of medicine was first conferred by this
college at the commencement in June, 1771, on four students who had
taken the bachelor's degree in 1768. The inaugural theses were then
required to be written in the Latin language and published in accordance with the rule established in 1767.

The medical department of the Philadelphia College, as now fully
organized and under the rules we have quoted, continued its regular
annual course of instruction with a steadily increasing reputation until
the city of Philadelphia was occupied by the British army in 1777.
The principal exception in regard to regularity was the omission of Dr.
Morgan's course during the winter of 1772-'73, on account of his absence
in the West Indies, where he appears to have gone for the purpose of
soliciting funds for the college. Owing to the disturbed state of society
during the first years of the war for independence, the number of students attending the college, and especially the number applying for
degrees, was less than during the first three or four years after the college was opened.

The session of 1776-'77 was broken up and the more valuable movable
materials of the college were privately removed to places of safety by
the provost and members of the faculty. Most of the medical professors
filled important places in connection with the American Army. Drs.
Morgan and Shippen successively acted as medical director general, and

Dr. Rush was medical director of the middle department, and was one of the signers of the Declaration of Independence, while Dr. Bond rendered important aid in the establishment and direction of military hospitals.

THE MEDICAL COLLEGE AND THE UNIVERSITY.

An attempt was made to resume the courses of medical instruction in the college in 1779, but owing to political differences and suspicions the charter was abrogated by an act of the State legislature dated November 27, 1779, the officers removed, and its property transferred to a new institution.*

This successor of the Philadelphia College, with a liberal charter and larger endowments, was called the University of the State of Pennsylvania.

Rev. John Ewing, D. D., was appointed to be provost, and an effort was immediately made to organize the medical department by offering those who had held professorships in the college the same positions in connection with the new university. Dr. William Shippen, jr., was the only one, however, who at once accepted the offer, and the trustees of the university, finding themselves unable to fill the other places satisfactorily, passed a resolution requesting the former medical professors of the college to examine such candidates for graduation as might apply to them for that purpose. This request appears to have been complied with, and at the public commencement held June 27, 1780, the degree of bachelor of medicine was conferred on William W. Smith and Ebenezer Crossby, and that of doctor of medicine on David Ramsay, who was in the service of the American Army, and at the time a prisoner in the hands of the British.

Although the abrogation of the charter of the College of Philadelphia deprived it of a legal existence, and the refusal of most of its former medical faculty to accept chairs in the university left the latter without an adequate number of teachers, yet regular annual courses of medical instruction continued to be given by Drs. Thomas Bond, William Shippen, jr., Benjamin Rush, and Adam Kuhn, and a few medical degrees were conferred at each annual commencement of the university.

The officers and friends of the College of Philadelphia, however, continued to regard the act abrogating its charter and confiscating its property as illegal and unjust; and in 1783 it was reorganized by a new election of trustees and faculty, and an effort was made to induce the legislature to repeal the former act.

In 1785 Dr. Benjamin Franklin, who had been one of the founders of the college, returned from his service as foreign minister, and was chosen president of the newly elected board of trustees. He lent the whole force of his influence in aid of his old colleagues and in favor of such legislation as would restore to the college its charter and property. Under such advocacy the legislature of the State was finally induced, in March, 1789

---

to repeal the act of abrogation and restore the college to all its rights and privileges, but leaving the university in existence with its endowment from confiscated estates the same as before. As soon as the act of restoration was passed the board of trustees of the college proceeded to again organize all its departments. Rev. Dr. Smith was reëlected provost, and all the medical professors were invited to resume their respective professorships, as held at the time of the abrogation of the charter nearly ten years previous. The invitation met with a cordial response; but the death of Dr. John Morgan, in October, 1789, and the resignation of Dr. Adam Kuhn in the same month, led to such changes that the medical faculty of the college, as fully formed in November of that year, contained the following names:

William Shippen, jr., M. D., professor of anatomy, surgery, and midwifery.

Benjamin Rush, M. D., professor of theory and practice of physic.

Caspar Wistar, M. D., professor of chemistry and of the institutes of physic.

Samuel P. Griffitts, M. D., professor of materia medica and pharmacy.

Benjamin Smith Barton, M. D., professor of natural history and botany.

In the meantime Dr. Shippen continued to hold the same chairs in the University of Pennsylvania; Dr. James Hutchinson, that of chemistry; and Dr. Adam Kuhn, that of theory and practice of medicine. Two institutions were thus brought into a fair and active competition in a field affording, at that time, a patronage too limited for one.

The trustees of the College of Philadelphia not only reinstated a full corps of medical professors, but they revised their former rules in regard to medical requirements. These rules, as adopted in 1767, provided for the conferring of the degree of bachelor as well as that of doctor of medicine. The student was permitted to apply for the first, after "a sufficient apprenticeship to some reputable practitioner in physic," attendance on "at least one course of lectures in anatomy, materia medica, chemistry, the theory and practice of physic, one course of clinical lectures, and attendance on the practice of the Pennsylvania Hospital one year." It was expected by the founders of the college that those who took the bachelor's degree would return after three years of study and practice and take the higher degree of doctor. But experience proved this expectation fallacious, as very few of those who entered into practice after receiving the first degree ever returned for the second. For this and other reasons the bachelor's degree was abolished, and the revised regulations adopted by the trustees of the college, November 17, 1789, and published in the Pennsylvania Gazette, were as follows:

1. No person shall be received as a candidate for the degree of doctor of medicine until he has arrived at the age of twenty-one years, and has applied himself to the study of medicine in the college for at least two years. Those students candidates who reside in the city of Philadelphia, or within five miles thereof, must have been the pupils of some respectable practitioner for the space of three years, and those who may

come from the country, and from any greater distance than five miles, must have studied with reputable physicians there for at least two years.

2. Every candidate shall have regularly attended the lectures of the following professors, viz : of anatomy and surgery ; of chemistry and the institutes of medicine ; of materia medica and pharmacy ; of the theory and practice of medicine ; the botanical lectures of the professor of natural history and botany ; and a course of lectures on natural and experimental philosophy.

3. Each candidate shall signify his intention of graduating to the dean of the medical faculty at least two months before the time of graduation, after which he shall be examined privately by the professors of the different branches of medicine. If remitted to his studies the professors shall hold themselves bound not to divulge the same ; but if he is judged to be properly qualified, a medical question and a case shall then be proposed to him, the answer and treatment of which he shall submit to the medical professors. If these performances are approved, the candidate shall then be admitted to a public examination before the trustees, the provost, vice provost, professors, and students of the college ; after which he shall offer to the inspection of each of the medical professors a thesis, written in the Latin or English language; (at his own option,) on a medical subject. This thesis, approved of, is to be printed at the expense of the candidate, and defended from such objections as may be made to it by the medical professors at a commencement to be held for the purpose of conferring degrees on the first Wednesday of June every year.

Bachelors in medicine who wish to be admitted to the degree of doctor in medicine shall publish and defend a thesis agreeably to the rules above mentioned.

The different medical lectures shall commence annually on the first Monday in November, the lectures in natural and experimental philosophy about the same time, and the lectures on botany on the first Monday in April.

BENJAMIN FRANKLIN,
President of Board of Trustees.
WILLIAM SMITH,
*Provost of the College and Secretary of Board of Trustees.**

The trustees of the University of Pennsylvania adopted very similar regulations regarding courses of lectures and time of study for the degree of doctor in medicine, but they continued also to confer the degree of bachelor, as before.

One hundred and four medical students were in attendance on the lectures during the college term of 1790–'91, and appear to have been nearly equally divided between the two schools.

The disadvantages arising from a division of the patronage between the two collegiate institutions were too apparent to be overlooked, and friends of both before long instituted measures for an amicable union. The efforts made resulted in the passage of an act by the legislature of the State, September 30, 1791, uniting the college and university on terms which had been previously agreed to by both the parties in interest. The name adopted for the united institution was the University of Pennsylvania. Dr. John Ewing was elected provost and professor of natural and experimental philosophy, and all the professors in the medical departments of the two previous institutions were elected professors in the new one.

The full medical faculty of the university, as thus constituted, was arranged as follows:

---

*History of University of Pennsylvania, by Joseph Carson, M. D., pp. 95, 96.

William Shippen, jr., M. D., professor of anatomy, surgery, and midwifery.

Caspar Wistar, M. D., adjunct.

Adam Kuhn, M. D., professor of the theory and practice of medicine.

Benjamin Rush, M. D., professor of institutes of medicine and clinical medicine.

James Hutchinson, M. D., professor of chemistry.

Samuel P. Griffitts, M. D., professor of materia medica and pharmacy.

Benjamin Smith Barton, M. D., professor of botany and natural history.

The university, as now reorganized, ceased to confer the degree of bachelor of medicine, and left it optional with the medical students whether they should attend the lectures on natural history and botany, but in all other respects adopted the "rules respecting a medical education and the conferring of degrees in medicine" which we have already given as adopted by the trustees of the College of Philadelphia in 1789.

Dr. Rush, in an introductory lecture to his course, commenced in November following the enactment of the legislature consolidating the two colleges under the name of the University of Pennsylvania, commented as follows: "I should do violence to my own feelings should I proceed to the subjects of the ensuing course of lectures without first congratulating you upon the union of the two medical schools of Philadelphia, under a charter founded upon the most liberal concessions by the gentlemen who projected it, and upon the purest principles of patriotism in the legislature of our State. By means of this event the ancient harmony of the different professors of medicine will be restored, and their united efforts will be devoted with accumulated force towards the advancement of our science."

We have thus sketched as briefly as is consistent with clearness the progress of medical instruction from its beginnings in Philadelphia to the complete establishment of the University of Pennsylvania by the formal election of the faculty as above named, in January, 1792; but more in detail than we deem it desirable to treat other colleges, for the reason that this one has served so largely as the model after which all our medical colleges have been formed, and because this institution continued to occupy a leading position in the work of medical education until the present time.

OTHER EARLY MEDICAL SCHOOLS.

While the cause of medical education was thus progressing in Philadelphia, the profession in New York was not idle. The zealous efforts of Drs. Bard, Middleton, and others, aided by a spirit of rivalry with Philadelphia, effected the organization of the Society of the New York Hospital, and procured for it a charter from the colonial government in 1767. The first hospital building, which had been nearly completed but

was not ready for occupancy, was destroyed by fire in 1772. This, with
the early and long continued occupation of the city by the British army,
prevented all renewal of the work until the close of the war for independence. Work was resumed after peace was restored and suitable
buildings were ready for the reception of patients in 1791. The institution continued under the control of the Society of the New York Hospital and a board of governors, and remained until the last few years one
of the most important public hospitals in this country. Its origin was
largely due to the efforts of Drs. Samuel Bard and Peter Middleton,
through whose personal labors were added liberal pecuniary contributions
for the erection of the first building, from the provincial governor, Sir
Henry Moore, the corporation of the city, the legislature of the province,
and many private citizens. Except the valuable lot on which it stood,
all this was lost by the fire that destroyed the building as it approached
completion. The efforts of the same parties to organize a medical school
in connection with King's College, which had been established in the
city of New York several years previously, were, however, attended with
better success. A full medical faculty was organized in 1768, composed
of Samuel Clossy, M. D., professor of anatomy; John Jones, M. D.,
professor of surgery; Peter Middleton, M. D., professor of physiology
and pathology; James Smith, M. D., professor of chemistry and materia
medica; John V. B. Tennent, M. D., professor of midwifery; and Samuel Bard, M. D., professor of theory and practice of physic. The first
courses of lectures were given 'in the autumn and winter of 1768–'69, at
the close of which, 'in May, 1769, the degree of bachelor in medicine was
conferred by the trustees of the college on Samuel Kissam and Robert
Tucker; and at the close of the succeeding college term, in May, 1770, the
degree of doctor in medicine was conferred upon one or both of the same
parties. These are stated by Dr. J. B. Beck and several other writers to
have been the first medical degrees conferred by colleges in America.*
This is correct, however, only as it relates to the degree of doctor of
medicine; for, as we have already stated, the College of Philadelphia
conferred the degree of bachelor of medicine on ten students at the
college commencement in June, 1768, but did not confer its first degree
of doctor of medicine until June, 1771. We have been unable to procure
a copy of the regulations adopted by the medical department of King's
College, or the requisites for graduation, but from the fact of conferring
both degrees, and other indications, it is evident that the conditions did
not differ materially from those relating to the same subject in the medical department of the College of Philadelphia.

The prosperity of the institution, however, was not at first commensu-
rate with the known respectability and learning of its professors; for N.
Romayne, M. D., informs us that, in 1774, six years after its organization,
only "about twenty-five persons attended the anatomical lectures, some

---

* See History of American Medicine before the Revolution, by J. B. Beck, M. D., in
Transactions of New York State Medical Society, vol. 5, p. 141.

of whom were students from the West Indies." This want of patronage has been attributed to the conduct of the trustees or governors of the college, but with what justice we are entirely unable to determine. It is more likely, however, that the disturbed state of the public mind, caused by the controversies of the colonies with the mother country, and the near approach of actual war, had more to do with the retarding of its prosperity than any other causes; and as New York was one of the earliest localities actually occupied by the British in the military conflict, the operations of the medical school were entirely suspended, and the members of the faculty became separated, some to responsible duties in the medical department of the American Army, and before the close of the strife some were cut off by death. Soon after the close of the war and the evacuation of the city by the British army, attempts were made to revive the medical department of King's (the name of which had, in the mean time, been changed to that of Columbia) College. Through some mismanagement the attempt not only failed, but was attended by circumstances that gave rise to a strong popular outbreak, commonly called the " doctors' mob." This arose from a suspicion that some bodies had been stolen from the graveyard for dissection. The rabble broke into the dissecting room of the college, and finding several subjects partially anatomized they exhibited the fragments to the multitude without, which so increased the excitement that all law and order were trampled under foot for two or three days. Several medical gentlemen were grossly insulted, and a few of the students were, for a brief period, confined in prison for personal safety.

To counteract as far as possible the evil influences brought to bear upon the profession, to serve the poor, and to improve medical science, several of the more enlightened young members formed themselves into a society, and in 1787 they succeeded in inducing the magistrates of the city to establish an apothecary shop at the public expense, and freely gave their professional services to the sick poor; in other words, they procured the establishment of what would now be called a public free dispensary. Among the more prominent engaged in this enterprise were William Moore, M. D., Nicholas Romayne, M. D., Benjamin Kissam, M. D., Wright Post, M. D., and Valentine Seaman, M. D. They not only bestowed gratuitous attendance on the poor, but added therewith lectures on most of the branches of medicine, thus constituting this dispensary the first institution connected with practical instruction in medicine under the corporation of the city. So great was their success that in 1790 more than fifty students attended.

Encouraged by this success, an attempt was made to organize an independent school under the name of the College of Physicians and Surgeons. This not proving successful at the time, another effort was made to revive the medical department of Columbia College.* In the autumn of 1791 the private association, under the superintendence of Nicholas

---

Romayne, introduced no fewer than sixty medical students into the college, and thereby prevailed on the legislature of the State to make a grant of $30,000 to the trustees for the purpose of enabling them to enlarge their buildings, &c. In the following year the medical faculty was reorganized with Richard Bayley, M. D., Wright Post, M. D., Samuel Rogers, M. D., William Hammersly, M. D., Henry Nicoll, M. D., and Benjamin Kissam, M. D., as professors, and Samuel Bard, M. D., as dean of the faculty. Some of these appointments were so unsatisfactory to the students that many of them abandoned the college and erased their names from the register. Indeed, such were the internal jealousies and outward prejudices, that the institution, though it maintained an existence until 1810, never attained a degree of prosperity equal to the private association to which we have alluded.

Toward the close of the war for independence, the subject of medical instruction began to attract attention in the New England States. In 1782 John Warren, M. D., commenced courses of lectures on anatomy, which were continued several years, and were attended by many of the students in Harvard College. Some liberal donations to the college from wealthy and enlightened friends of medical instruction were made about this time, and in 1783 the college organized a regular faculty consisting of John Warren, M. D., professor of anatomy and surgery; Aaron Dexter, M. D., professor of chemistry and materia medica; and Benjamin Waterhouse, M. D., professor of theory and practice of medicine.* This organization was popular and attracted the attendance of a small class of medical students annually until 1810, when the medical department was moved from Cambridge to Boston, where it soon attained a higher degree of prosperity, and has since continued the leading medical school in the Eastern States.

The medical department of Dartmouth College, at Hanover, N. H., was organized in 1797, chiefly through the influence of Nathan Smith, M. D., who was appointed professor of medicine, and for ten or twelve years taught all the branches with signal ability. Only a small number of students attended during the first few years after its opening, the degree of bachelor of medicine having been conferred on from one to eight candidates annually, but only one receiving the higher degree of doctor during the whole period.

The very limited degree of prosperity enjoyed by the medical school of Columbia College, in New York, led many members of the profession in that city to use their influence in favor of the establishment of another and independent medical college. In accordance with their wishes, the regents of the University of the State of New York granted a charter for a new college in 1807, to be located in the city, and called the College of Physicians and Surgeons of New York. This school was placed

---

* Dr. Ezekiel Hersey, of Hingham, bequeathed £1,000 and his widow a like sum, for the support of a professor of anatomy and surgery. In 1786 Abner Hersey, M. D., of Barnstable, and John Cuming, M. D., of Concord, gave each £500 for the same purpose.—(Thacher's Medical Biography, p. 31.)

under the control of a board of trustees consisting of the whole Medical Society of the City and County of New York, and the degree of doctor of medicine was conferred by the regents of the university of the State on the recommendation of the trustees and faculty of the college. The first course of lectures was given in the winter of 1807–'8 to a class of fifty-three students.

In 1810 the medical department of Columbia College was finally discontinued, leaving the College of Physicians and Surgeons the only one in the State, with a class of students numbering eighty-two, and the following able faculty:

Samuel Bard, M. D., president.

David Hosack, M. D., vice president and professor of the theory and practice of physic and clinical medicine.

William James McNeven, M. D., professor of chemistry.

Samuel L. Mitchell, M. D., professor of materia medica and botany.

Valentine Mott, M. D., professor of surgery.

John W. Francis, M. D., professor of obstetrics and diseases of women and children.

Wright Post, M. D., professor of anatomy.

The rapid prosperity which the friends of the institution and the regents of the university anticipated was not realized. The very numerous board of trustees, being mostly medical practitioners in the immediate vicinity of the college, soon became distracted by opposing counsels and jealousies which, extending to the members of the faculty, caused much difficulty, and greatly retarded the prosperity of the college and the progress of medicine in that city.

The medical department of the University of Maryland, at Baltimore, was incorporated in 1807,* and was at once supplied with an able faculty, consisting of John B. Davidge, M. D., professor of principles and practice of surgery, and Nathaniel Potter, M. D., professor of the theory and practice of medicine, assisted by John Shaw, M. D., of Maryland, and James Cocke, M. D., of Virginia. This institution met with fair success, preserved its organization, and is among the leading colleges of the country.

RÉSUMÉ AND GENERAL REMARKS.

By the foregoing brief sketch it will be seen that during the first thirty years after the close of the war for independence, which included the first decade of the present century, seven medical colleges were organized and located as follows: two in Philadelphia, two in New York, one in Boston, one in Hanover, N. H., and one in Baltimore. The two in Philadelphia were speedily merged into one, and one of those in New York was discontinued in a few years. We find, therefore, only five medical schools in

---

* As early as 1804 John B. Davidge commenced a course of lectures on midwifery, which he extended so as to include anatomy and surgery, to a class of six students in the city of Baltimore.

existence in the United States in 1810, with an aggregate number of medical students in attendance of about 650, of whom about 100 received either the degree of bachelor or doctor of medicine. Two-thirds of the whole number were in the University of Pennsylvania. Only three public general hospitals had been established, namely, Pennsylvania Hospital, in Philadelphia; the New York Hospital, in New York City; and the Charity Hospital, in New Orleans.* The first proved a very important aid to the University of Pennsylvania in attracting medica' students to Philadelphia by the clinical instruction which it afforded, as inaugurated by Dr. Thomas Bond, soon after it was opened for the reception of patients.

With a single exception, these medical schools were organized as departments of universities or colleges of literature and science previously established; and all but this one began with a small number of professors, making it necessary that one should teach two and sometimes three branches of medicine during each annual college term. For this reason more than any other the medical college terms were made to commence generally in October and continue until the following May or June.

All these schools adopted at first the policy of conferring the degree of bachelor of medicine on students who had studied medicine with some respectable practitioner not less than two years and attended all the medical instructions in the college one year, or rather one college term; and the degree of doctor of medicine after three years of study and two annual college terms. It must be remembered that during the colonial period of our history, and for thirty or forty years subsequent to the achievement of our national independence, it was the universal custom for young men who entered upon the study of medicine to become regularly apprenticed to some practitioner for a term of three or four years during which time the preceptor was entitled to the student's services in preparing and dispensing medicines, extracting teeth, bleeding, and other minor surgical operations, and, when more advanced in studies, in attending on the sick; as a return for this he was obliged to give the student detailed and thorough instruction in all the branches of medicine. Many of the more eminent practitioners frequently had several students in their offices at one time, constituting a small class, who were drilled as regularly in their studies as they would be in college. In some instances the term of apprenticeship was extended to six and seven years, and was made to commence at the early age of fifteen or sixteen years. All these customs were brought by the immigrants from the parent country, and their perpetuation here was rendered

---

* In 1781, Don Andres Almonester commenced the erection of a public general hospital in the city of New Orleans on the site of the one blown down in the great storm of 1779. It was called the New Charity Hospital, and cost $114,000. As Louisiana became one of the States of our Union, by purchase, in 1803, this hospital must be recognized with those of Philadelphia and New York.

more necessary by the sparseness of the population and the difficulty of access to medical schools.*

In the midst of such customs, and at a period in the world's history when railroads, steamboats, and other means of speedy transit were unknown, and even post coaches were rare, it was entirely reasonable that the first idea of a medical college should be to furnish the means for a rapid review of the several branches of medical science, aided by such experiments and appliances for illustration as could be commanded, and the whole concentrated into as small a part of the year as possible. The idea of the founders of medical schools, both in Great Britain and in this country, was to make them supplement, but not supersede, the work of the preceptor and the medical apprentice. The study of anatomy by dissections, the illustration of chemistry by experiments, the clinical observations of disease at the bedside, were capable of being carried on in the offices of preceptors only to a very limited extent. But by combining several preceptors, each eminently qualified in some one department, in a college faculty, with access to anatomical rooms, chemical laboratory, and hospital for the sick, all the branches of medicine then recognized could be very well reviewed, in the form of didactic instruction, in five or six months of the year. It was expressly to supply the wants here indicated, with the greatest economy of time and labor, that the medical department of the University of Elinburgh was founded in the beginning of the eighteenth century. Conferring its first degree of doctor in medicine in the year 1705, it rose rapidly to distinction among the schools of Europe, and furnished the model after which all the first medical schools in this country were organized, as it was the alma mater of nearly all their first professors. Assuming that the student would serve from two to four years of his apprenticeship to his preceptor before resorting to a medical school, the several professors very naturally arranged their courses of instruction to begin nearly at the same time, generally in September or October, and to be completed in time for the public commencement and conferring of degrees in the following May or June; and as the bachelor's degree was generally conferred after attendance on one full course of college instruction in the several branches taught, no gradation or consecutive order of studies could be incorporated into the college course. The addition of one or two years more of study, including a second course of college instruction, entitled the applicant to an examination for the degree of doctor of medicine. At the first organization of all the medical schools to which I have thus far alluded, provision was made for conferring the degrees of both bachelor and doctor of medicine. But, as already mentioned, the degree of bachelor was abandoned by the College of Philadelphia in 1789, and by the University of Pennsylvania in 1791, and by all the medical colleges in this country after 1813. The whole number of medical

---

degrees conferred by the seven medical schools whose origin is here traced, prior to 1810, probably did not exceed six hundred.

Very many, however, served their regular apprenticeship with a preceptor, attended one course of college instruction, and entered upon practice without a college degree; and there were not a few who entered upon the responsible duties of practice with the simple certificate of their preceptor, without ever seeing the inside of a college.

We shall not fully appreciate the relations of the medical schools to the needs of the profession, in the early days of the Republic, unless we consider also the coincident condition of the different branches of medical science. To the active workers of the present generation, a medical college with only three or four professors, or with one professor attempting to teach anatomy, surgery, and midwifery, all in one college term of five or six months, would appear hardly less than absurd. If we remember, however, that down to the commencement of the present century the principal medical works in use were the writings of Sydenham, Bœrhaave, and Cullen; the physiology of Haller; the anatomy of Cheselden and Munro; the surgery of Sharp, Pott, and Jones; the midwifery of Hunter and Smellie; and the materia medica of Lewis, we shall readily see that the field of medical study was limited in comparison to that which now opens before the student. At that time surgery had only begun to be recognized as a department distinct from anatomy. We learn from an introductory lecture by James Spence, F. R. C. S. E., professor in the University of Edinburgh, that "so late as 1777, when the college of surgeons petitioned the patrons to institute a separate professorship of surgery in the university, they were opposed by Munro, then professor of anatomy, as interfering with his subject; and he succeeded in getting his commission altered so as to include surgery, which was thus made a mere adjunct of the anatomical course, and continued to be so taught (if it could be said to be taught) until the institution of the chair of surgery in 1831." It was not until June 4, 1805, that surgery was separated from the chair of anatomy, by the appointment of Philip Syng Physick, M. D., as professor of surgery, on an equality with the other professorships, in the University of Pennsylvania. The department of midwifery was still later in gaining recognition as a distinct branch of medicine. At the request of Caspar Wistar, M. D., who had succeeded to the professorship of anatomy and midwifery in the university on the death of Dr. Shippen, in 1803, the trustees separated the chairs, and in 1810 appointed Thomas Chalkley James, M. D., the first professor of midwifery in that college. And yet it was not until three years later, October 11, 1813, that he was formally recognized as a full member of the faculty, and attendance on his lectures rendered obligatory upon the students who applied for a degree. In New York, however, midwifery was recognized as a distinct branch at a much earlier period than in any of the other cities in which medical schools had been organized; for in the first medical faculty appointed in connection with

King's College, in 1768, Dr. John V. B. Tennent was made professor of midwifery, apparently on an equal footing with all the other professors.

The foregoing facts are sufficient to show the limited field of medical science cultivated at the beginning of the present century, compared with the same field at the present time. If this is borne in mind, it will be seen that the 5 medical schools—embracing the medical departments of the University of Pennsylvania ; of Harvard University, removed in 1810 to Boston ; of Dartmouth College, at Hanover; of the University of Maryland, at Baltimore; and of the College of Physicians and Surgeons of New York—which were either reorganized or founded *de novo* during the first thirty years of our history as an independent nation, were established on as liberal a basis, and were as well adapted to the then existing wants of the profession and the people, as any that have been organized since. As a general rule they commenced with a small number of professors, but as the different departments of professional knowledge became better developed, and the work of instruction more thoroughly systematized, there was shown that tendency to make divisions of labor by the creation of new chairs which has continued to the present time.

In this respect the University of Pennsylvania, as the leading school, may be taken as a representative of all the rest. Commencing with only two professors, Drs. Morgan and Shippen, aided by the clinical instruction of Dr. Bond in the hospital, in 1765, the number was increased by the addition of chairs of chemistry and materia medica in 1768–'69, and on the merging of the College of Philadelphia with the University of Pennsylvania, in 1791–'92, the number of chairs was increased to six by the addition of professorships of institutes of medicine and of botany and natural history. A further addition took place by the creation of an independent chair of surgery in 1805, and one of midwifery in 1810.

MEDICAL SCHOOLS ESTABLISHED OR ORGANIZED SINCE 1810.

During the year 1810, a medical department was established in connection with Yale College, in New Haven, but the first course of lectures was not commenced until three years later. It was organized on the same plan as the schools connected with Harvard and Dartmouth. The first class of medical students for the college term of 1813–'14 numbered 37, of whom three received the degree of doctor of medicine at the commencement in 1814. The first faculty in this school was headed by Dr. Nathan Smith, who had already gained a high reputation as the professor of medicine in the medical department of Dartmouth College. He was appointed professor of the theory and practice of physic, surgery, and obstetrics, with Dr. Eli Ives professor of materia medica and botany, and lecturer on diseases of women and children, and Dr. Benjamin Silliman, professor of chemistry, pharmacy, mineralogy, and geology, as colleagues. To these were soon after added Dr. Jonathan

Knight, professor of anatomy and physiology, and lecturer on obstetrics, and Æneas Munson, M. D., professor of institutes of medicine. With this able faculty the school rapidly acquired reputation and a fair share of professional patronage. As proof of this we find the number of medical students attending the college term of 1822–'23 to have been 92, of whom 28 received the degree of doctor of medicine at the close of the term.

In 1812 the regents of the University of New York incorporated a second medical college under the name of the College of Physicians and Surgeons of the Western District of the State of New York. It was located at Fairfield, Herkimer County, a small village then on the western borders of civilization. The legislature of the State appropriated $15,000 to aid in the erection of suitable buildings, and the first course of instruction was given in 1813–'14 to a class of 33 students. The first professors appointed were Lyman Spalding, M. D., who had been a pupil of and assistant to Nathan Smith, M. D., of Dartmouth College, Westel Willoughby, M. D., James Hadley, M. D., and John Stearns, M. D. The first was appointed president of the faculty and professor of anatomy and surgery and lecturer on institutes of medicine; the second, professor of obstetrics and diseases of women and children; the third, professor of chemistry and materia medica; and the fourth, professor of theory and practice of physic. Dr. Spalding soon after removed to the city of New York, and, finding it inconvenient to divide his time between the two places, resigned, and was succeeded in the presidency and the chair of surgery by Joseph White, M. D., of Cherry Valley, while the chair of anatomy and physiology was given to James McNaughton, M. D., and that of the theory and practice of medicine and medical jurisprudence was assigned to T. Romeyn Beck, M. D., the two latter of Albany. On the death of Dr. White, in 1832, his chair was filled for a short time by one of his sons, and subsequently by John Delamater, M. D. At a still later period Dr. Willoughby, having reached a ripe age and an enviable reputation, resigned, and Reuben D. Mussey, M. D., was elected a member of the faculty in 1836. Under the influence and labors of these eminent men the school attained a good reputation, and was attended by classes numbering from 114 to 217, until 1840, when the whole faculty resigned on account of the opening of medical colleges in Albany and Geneva under charters granted by the State legislature, by which the patronage would be so divided as to give neither of the schools a reasonable support. From that date the College of Physicians and Surgeons of the Western District ceased to exist. During the twenty-seven years of its history it afforded instruction to 3,123 students, and graduated 589.

In 1818 Theodore Woodward, M. D., of Castleton, Vt., aided by Selah Gridley, M.D., succeeded in organizing a medical college in that town under the name of the Vermont Academy of Medicine. It received a charter from the legislature of that State, in 1835, and the faculty, when organized, consisted of—

William Tully, M. D., president and professor of the theory and practice of physic and medical jurisprudence.

Theodore Woodward, M. D., professor of the principles and practice of surgery, obstetrics, and diseases of women and children.

Alden March, M. D., professor of anatomy and physiology.

Jonathan A. Allen, M. D., professor of materia medica and pharmacy.

Lewis C. Beck, M. D., professor of chemistry and natural history.

Amos Eaton, esq., professor of natural philosophy.

The first course of lectures was given in 1818 to 24 students. The degree of doctor of medicine was conferred by the Middlebury College, on the recommendation of the medical faculty, until 1827, after which it was conferred directly by the faculty under its amended charter. In 1835 the faculty of this school commenced giving two separate courses of instruction each year, one commencing in the autumn and one in the spring. The school enjoyed a moderate degree of prosperity until 1837, when its courses of instruction were suspended for a few years.* At a subsequent period the faculty was reorganized and regular instruction was resumed, and continued until 1854; it graduated in all 350 students.†

In 1817 a medical school was fully organized as a department of the Transylvania University, Lexington, Ky., chiefly through the influence of B. W. Dudley, W. H. Richardson, and James Blythe. Many attempts had been made to fill the various chairs of medicine in this institution, from the appointment of Samuel Brown, M. D., in 1799, to the professorship of anatomy, surgery, and chemistry. In 1801, Frederick Ridgley, M. D., was elected professor of medicine. In 1805, James Fishback, M. D., was appointed to the chair of theory and practice. Walter Warfield, M. D., was made professor of midwifery and surgery in 1809. The faculty was recast and another effort was made to open the medical department in 1809; still another one, with new encouragement in 1815 but without success until 1817–'18, when the faculty was organized by the appointment of Benjamin W. Dudley, M. D., professor of anatomy and surgery; Daniel Drake, M. D., professor of materia medica; William H. Richardson, M. D., professor of obstetrics and diseases of women and children; James Blythe, M. D., professor of chemistry; and Samuel Brown, M. D., professor of theory and practice of medicine. Twenty students attended the first course of lectures, only one of whom received the degree of doctor of medicine at the commencement. At the close of this term Dr.

---

* See Statistics of Medical Colleges, in Transactions of Medical Society of the State of New York, by T. R. Beck, M. D., 1840.

† This college had throughout its existence a most excellent faculty, and proved to be a great feeder of the medical institutions of Philadelphia and New York. The class during the last year numbered 91 matriculates.

Drake resigned and returned to Cincinnati, but again filled the same chair in 1823, and on the resignation of Dr. Brown in 1825 he was transferred to the chair of theory and practice of medicine; C. W. Short, M. D., was elected professor of materia medica and medical botany; and Charles Caldwell, M. D., to the chair of institutes of medicine and clinical medicine. As thus organized the faculty imparted to the school a high reputation, and attracted to its halls large classes; that for the college term of 1825–'26 numbering 281, 65 of whom graduated at the close of the term. Although many changes took place in the faculty, the prosperity of the school was maintained for twenty-five years, after which it rapidly declined and at length ceased to exist.*

When Dr. Daniel Drake left the Transylvania University, in the spring of 1818, he immediately commenced his efforts to organize a medical college in Cincinnati. An act passed the State legislature in January, 1819, incorporating the Medical College of Ohio. He succeeded in organizing a faculty, with himself in the chair of practical medicine, and a course of instruction was given to a small class of students during the autumn and winter of 1819–'20. Sharp differences soon sprang up between Dr. Drake and his colleagues, in consequence of which he was compelled to leave the school. As subsequently organized, the faculty consisted of Jedediah Cobb, M. D., professor of institutes and practice of medicine; Jesse Smith, M. D., professor of anatomy and surgery; John Moorhead, M. D., professor of materia medica and medical obstetrics; and Elijah Slack, M. D., professor of chemistry and pharmacy. The school thus founded acquired reputation slowly but permanently, though in the midst of much professional rivalry and opposition, and has maintained its position to the present day. Among the more prominent medical teachers who have at different times been connected with its faculty, in addition to those already mentioned as its founders, may be named John Eberle, M. D., Thomas D. Mitchell, M. D., John P. Harrison, M. D., L. C. Rives, M. D., R. D. Mussey, M. D., and George C. Blackman, M. D.

*In 1820 the Medical School of Maine was organized as a department of Bowdoin College, at Brunswick, with three professorships, which were filled as follows: Nathan Smith, M. D., professor of theory and practice of physic and surgery; John D. Wells, M. D., professor of anatomy and physiology; and Parker Cleaveland, M. D., professor of chemistry and materia medica. The first course of lectures was given in 1821 to a class of twenty-one students, two of whom received the degree of M. D. Like the medical departments of Dartmouth and Yale, that of Bowdoin has maintained a stable and honorable progress until the present time, with classes varying from fifty to one hundred annually.

In 1821 a medical school was organized in connection with Brown University, at Providence, R. I., but was soon after discontinued.

The medical school of the University of Vermont was organized at Burlington in 1822. In 1827–'28 the faculty consisted of Henry S. Waterhouse, M. D., professor of surgery and obstetrics; William Sweetser, M. D., professor of the theory and practice of physic and of materia medica; George W. Benedict, A. M., professor of mathematics, natural philosophy, and chemistry; and John Bell, M. D., professor of anatomy and physiology. The school did not attract sufficient patronage to afford a fair support, and was discontinued after a few years. It was subsequently reorganized with a full faculty, and has continued to give instruction to small classes annually until the present time.

In 1823 a medical school was organized at Pittsfield, Mass., under the charter of Williams College, called the Berkshire Medical Institution. The establishment of this school was due chiefly to the influence of H. H. Childs, M. D., who had been an active and influential practitioner in that place for twenty years. On the first organization of the school he was appointed professor of the theory and practice of physic, and Chester Dewey, A. M., professor of chemistry, botany, mineralogy, and natural philosophy; and, in 1826–'27, their colleagues were John P. Batchelder, M. D., professor of surgery and physiology; John D. Wells, M. D., professor of anatomy and physiology; John Delamater, M. D., professor of pharmacy, materia medica, and obstetrics; and Stephen W. Williams, M. D., professor of medical jurisprudence. The first class of medical students in 1823 numbered 84, seven of whom graduated at the close of the college term. In 1825 the number in the class had increased to 112, and the graduates to 21. It thus early attained a good degree of prosperity, which was pretty steadily maintained for forty years, during nearly all of which time its founder, Prof. Henry H. Childs, continued to occupy the chair of practice. Whenever vacancies occurred in other chairs they were generally filled with men of ability, until 1867, when the college was closed. The building was subsequently purchased by the town authorities and occupied by a high and grammar school until April, 1876, when it was destroyed by fire.

In 1824 the Medical College of South Carolina was organized at Charleston. During the colonial period of our history South Carolina was peculiarly favored with physicians of a high order of attainment; and even after the close of the war for independence a larger proportion of her physicians were regular graduates of European colleges than in any other State. The names of John Lining, Lionel Chalmers, David Ramsay, Alexander Garden, James Moultrie, Alexander Baron, and Samuel Wilson will always make the early history of medicine in that State illustrious.

The faculty of the new college, when fully organized, consisted of the following:

James Ramsay, M. D., professor of surgery.

John Edwards Holbrook, M. D., professor of anatomy.

S. Henry Dickson, M. D., professor of the institutes and practice of physic.

Thomas G. Prioleau, M. D., professor of obstetrics and diseases of women and children.

Henry Rutledge Frost, M. D., professor of materia medica.

Edmund Ravenel, M. D., professor of chemistry.

Stephen Elliot, LL. D., professor of botany and natural history.

The Medical Society of the State of South Carolina had been organized under an act of the State legislature in 1817 with two boards of examiners, one in Charleston and the other in Columbia. The college was also placed under the control of the State society, much in the same way the College of Physicians and Surgeons of New York was under the control of the medical society of the county. The first course of instruction was given in the autumn and winter of 1824-'25 to a class of 50 students. The reputation and patronage of the college increased rapidly, the class of 1830-'31 numbering 131, 59 of whom graduated at the close of the term. In 1829 an additional chair, that of pathological and surgical anatomy, was created and filled by John Wagner, M. D. On the death of Dr. Ramsay, in 1832, Dr. Wagner was transferred to the chair of surgery, which he filled with credit until his death in 1841. But soon after the organization of the college, differences began to develop between the faculty and the State Medical Society as the governing body. These increased until, in 1832, the whole faculty resigned, and their places were filled by other persons. The old faculty immediately obtained an independent charter from the State legislature, and in the autumn of 1833 commenced a new college, called the Medical College of the State of South Carolina. The first class of students numbered 103, leaving a much smaller number in attendance in the older college. The latter after a few years was discontinued, while the former, under a charter independent of the State Medical Society continued to be one of the most prosperous in the country and stood high when its work was interrupted by the war of the rebellion in 1861. Soon after the close of the war the organization of the Medical College was revived, but chiefly with new men in the faculty. Several of those who had contributed so much to the high reputation of the school in the earlier part of its history were dead, and others had been pushed to other fields by the fortunes of war. The new faculty in 1874-'75 was composed as follows:

R. A. Kinloch, M. D., professor of the principles and practice of surgery and clinical surgery.

J. P. Chazal, M. D., professor of pathology and practice of medicine.

Middleton Michel, M. D., professor of physiology.

C. U. Shepard, jr., M. D., professor of chemistry.

F. L. Parker, M. D., professor of anatomy.

J. Ford Prioleau, M. D., professor of obstetrics and gynecology.

F. Peyre Porcher, M. D., professor of materia medica, therapeutics, and of clinical medicine.

Manning Simons, M. D., demonstrator of anatomy.

The medical department of Columbian College, in the District of Columbia, was organized in 1825, largely through the influence of Thomas Sewall, M. D., and Frederick May, M. D. This college was chartered by Congress in 1821, an d some appointments to the medical faculty were made the same year. Six professorships were established and filled as follows:

Thomas Sewall, M. D., professor of anatomy and physiology.

Thomas Henderson, M. D., professor of the theory and practice of medicine.

James M. Stoughton, M. D., professor of surgery.

Frederick May, M. D., professor of obstetrics.

N. W. Worthington, M. D., professor of materia medica.

Edward Cutbush, M. D., professor of chemistry.

The annual courses of instruction were given regularly for nine years to classes of medical students varying in number from 30 to 50, the whole number of graduates during that period being 81. The operations of the school were suspended from 1834 to 1838, but were resumed in the autumn of the latter year under the name of the National Medical College, yet still retaining the relation of medical department of what had now become Columbian University. Under this name and organization it has continued its annual courses of instruction, except for two years during the war, to classes varying from 28 to 55 in number until the present time.

From the reorganization of the University of Pennsylvania, after the close of the war for independence, to 1825, it was the only medical school in Philadelphia. Its unusual prosperity excited the envy as well as the admiration of many even of its own alumni, who became ambitious to excel as teachers in medicine.* Prominent among these were George McClellan and John Eberle, both of whom began to give private courses of medical instruction in that city between the years 1822 and 1825, and soon boldly advocated the establishment of another medical college. In the winter of 1825 a charter or law was passed by the legislature, under which the new medical school was organized in connection with Jefferson College, a flourishing literary institution at Cannonsburg, and hence the new medical school took the name of Jefferson Medical College. As nearly as we can ascertain, the first faculty consisted of the following members:

John Eberle, M. D., professor of the theory and practice of clinical medicine.

George McClellan, M. D., professor of surgery.

---

* The first effort to establish a second college in Philadelphia was in 1816. In the winter of 1818–'19, W. P. C. Barton, M. D., fitted up a lecture room attached to the rear of his residence, where he delivered lectures on materia medica and botany. This same year he petitioned the legislature of Pennsylvania for a charter for a medical school, but such influences were brought to bear that the movement was defeated. Measures were ripening, however, and others became interested in the cause, for a more vigorous and persistent effort.

Nathan R. Smith, M. D., professor of anatomy and physiology.

F. S. Beattie, M. D., professor of the institutes of medicine and midwifery.

B. Rush Rhees, M. D., professor of materia medica.

Jacob Green, A. M., professor of chemistry.

The first course of college instruction was commenced in the autumn of 1825 to a class of 110 students, 20 of whom received the degree of doctor of medicine at the close of the term. The work of establishing the new college not only encountered the active opposition of the faculty and more immediate friends of the University of Pennsylvania, but was also unpopular with a large majority of the profession in Philadelphia. Owing to these circumstances, and the warm controversies to which they gave rise, the classes of students did not increase, but rather the reverse, during the first five years. With the hope of increasing the reputation of the school, Dr. Daniel Drake, of Cincinnati, was engaged to give the course on practical medicine during the college term of 1830–'31. This expedient not only failed in its object, but resulted in the resignation of both Eberle and Drake and their return to the West during the succeeding year. Their places were immediately filled, and two years later the prosperity of the college began to increase rapidly, the class in attendance during the session of 1835–'36 numbering 364. Notwithstanding this, objections to its founder, Dr. McClellan, became so strong that in 1838 the board of trustees felt constrained to declare all the professorships vacant, and in refilling them omitted his name from the list. Subsequently the reputation of the school became largely identified with the names of Thomas Muter, J. K. Mitchell, C. D. Meigs, R. J. Dunglison, S. H. Dixon, and S. D. Gross, and it has kept to the present time in the front rank of American medical colleges.

The medical department of the University of Virginia, at Charlottesville, was chartered by the State in the year 1819, and organized in the year 1825. The organization of this school differed in some important respects from that of all the other medical colleges in the country. Instead of having a full faculty of six or seven professors, and giving its instruction in didactic lectures extending only through four or five months of each year, the faculty was made to consist of only four professors, the annual term of instruction nine months, and the method of teaching was by recitations and demonstrations, as in other departments of scientific and literary study. The general arrangement of classes and professorships will be understood from the university catalogue for 1875–'76, which says: "The length of the session (nine months) renders it convenient and eligible to distribute the subjects of instruction among a smaller number of professors than in the other medical schools of the United States, whose sessions are only four or five months long. Thus, to one professor are assigned physiology and surgery; to another, human anatomy and materia medica; to a third, chemistry and pharmacy; and to a fourth, medical jurisprudence, obstetrics, and the practice of medicine. This distribution renders it practicable to bring the different subjects to the attention of the student in their natural and successive order. The arrangement of the lectures is such that he acquires a competent knowledge of anatomy, physiology, and chemistry before he enters upon the study of the principles and practice of medicine and surgery, which can only be studied properly in the lights shed upon them by the former." The graduation of the student is made to depend "upon satisfactory evidences of attainments only, without regard to the length of time he may have been attending the lectures."

The Medical School of the Valley of Virginia, or as it is more generally called, the Winchester Medical College, was organized at Winchester in 1826.* Like the medical department of the University of Virginia, it was organized on the plan of a long course of annual instruction with a small number of professors. The first faculty consisted of John G. Cooke, M. D., professor of the theory and practice of physic and obstetrics; Philip Smith, M. D., professor of materia medica; H. H. McGuire, M. D., professor of anatomy and physiology, and A. F. Magill, M. D., professor of surgery and chemistry. ·The annual college term continued from October 1 to June 1. The number of students in attendance was small and never subsequently increased sufficiently to give the school adequate support. It is not mentioned in the Statistics of Medical Colleges published by T. Romeyn Beck, M. D., in 1839, and although included in the list contained in the full report of Dr. F. C. Stewart to the American Medical Association in 1849, no statistics concerning the number of students or graduates are given by him. Since the war it has ceased to exist.

In 1827 the Washington Medical College was organized in Baltimore, Md., and the first course of instruction was given in the autumn and winter of 1827–'28. Its degrees were conferred by the Washington College in Pennsylvania, until 1833–'34, when it received an independent charter from the legislature of Maryland. The following facts are taken from a full history of the institution furnished, in manuscript, by John F. Monmonier, M. D. The faculty as first organized, in 1827, was composed of Horatio G. Jameson, M. D., professor of surgery; Samuel Annan, M. D., professor of anatomy; W. W. Handy, M. D., professor of obstetrics; Samuel R. Jennings, M. D., professor of materia medica; James H. Miller, M. D., professor of practice of medicine; and Henry Vethake, M. D., professor of chemistry. After the first course of lectures was completed the professor of chemistry resigned and Dr. James B. Rogers was elected to fill the vacancy. The faculty as thus organized continued regular annual courses of instruction to small classes until the reception of an independent charter in 1833, when they undertook to erect new college buildings sufficient to accommodate the work of the college, and room for hospital patients for clinical purposes. During the progress of this work Professors Annan, Rogers, and Jame-

---

* Thacher's American Medical Biography, p. 75.

son resigned, and their places were filled by the election of J. C. S. Monkur, M. D., E. Foreman, M. D., and J. R. W. Dunbar, M. D. The new college and hospital building was completed and occupied in October, 1836, but the classes of students did not increase in numbers, as had been expected from the better accommodations and clinical facilities, and consequently little or no progress was made in paying the debt contracted by the faculty in constructing the building. Consequently, after occupying it until 1848, it was abandoned to its creditors, and the college moved to another building.

In 1839 the legislature of Maryland passed an act supplementary to the original charter granted in 1833, by which university privileges were granted to the college, authorizing the organization of the three other faculties or colleges, namely, those of law, divinity, and arts and sciences, with such academic or preparatory schools as might be deemed essential to the support of said higher faculties. Nothing, however, was done under this supplementary charter, the medical faculty alone continuing its regular courses of instruction to small classes until 1853, when financial embarrassments had again accumulated to such a degree as to cause a suspension of all further active operations. During the interval from 1836 to 1853 the chair of surgery was occupied successively by Valentine Mott, M. D., George Bell Gibson, M. D., Reginald E. Wright, M. D., and W. Willis Baxley, M. D.; that of practice, by Thomas E. Bond, M. D., and John C. S. Monkur, M. D.; that of anatomy, by W. T. Leonard, M. D., and A. Snowden Piggott, M. D.; that of obstetrics, by G. C. M. Roberts, M. D.; and that of chemistry, by Reginald E. Wright, M. D. The original charter vested in the corporators, consisting of the members of the medical faculty and their successors, full power to control the institution in all its relations. It also provided a board of visitors, consisting of twenty-four members, with power to perpetuate their own organization and to advise in all matters relating to the interests of the college; but their action was merely advisory. There was no State or municipal control exercised over the institution, and no grants of public money or other pecuniary aid were given it, except for hospital purposes. In 1867 circumstances appeared favorable for reviving the college, which was done under the name of the Washington University. A building was secured, a dispensary for the poor opened, and the first course of lectures commenced on the first day of October, 1867. The new faculty consisted of Thomas E. Bond, M. D., president; G. C. M. Roberts, M. D., emeritus professor of obstetrics; A. J. Foard, M. D., professor of descriptive and surgical anatomy; J. P. Logan, M. D., professor of principles and practice of medicine; Harvey L. Byrd, M. D., professor of obstetrics; Martin P. Scott, M. D., professor of diseases of women and children; Edward Warren, M. D., professor of principles and practice of surgery; John F. Monmonier, M. D., professor of physiology; J. G. Moorman, M. D., professor of medical jurisprudence and hygiene; Joseph E. Clagett, M. D., professor

of materia medica and therapeutics; Clarence Morfit, M. D., professor
of medical chemistry and pharmacy; and John N. Monmonier, M. D.,
demonstrator of anatomy. The reputation of the faculty and the circumstances of the country were favorable for attracting students, especially
from the Southern States. The first class, consequently, numbered 149
students, 54 of whom graduated at the close of the term in February,
1868. In March, 1868, the legislature of Maryland passed an act appro-
priating $10,000 for the establishment of a hospital in connection
with the university. The comparatively large classes for 1867–'68 and
1868–'69 encouraged the faculty to erect a new college building and to
make themselves responsible for the necessary funds. To relieve them
from this embarrassment, however, the legislature made an appropriation
of $10,000, on the conditions that the faculty relinquish all claim to the
property and provide for the reception of beneficiary students. Under
this latter condition the faculty provided for the reception of one beneficiary student from each congressional district in the recent slavehold-
ing States; and in compliance with the conditions attached to an annual
appropriation of $2,500 for the support of the hospital, beneficiary
scholarships were offered to each senatorial district in the State of Maryland. Notwithstanding these helps and apparently liberal inducements
for patronage, frequent changes took place in the personnel of the
faculty, and the number of students gradually declined from 155 in
1868–'69 to 70 in 1875–'76, and the graduates from 83 in the former year
to 32 in the latter.

The Medical College of Georgia, located at Augusta, was incorporated
by an act of the legislature of that State in 1831, and the first course of
instruction was given in 1832–'33. This college was organized, in 1828,
as an academy of medicine, by Milton M. Antony, M. D. Dr. Antony
was a man of learning and of enlarged views as to the sphere of duty
and the measure of responsibility of the college in elevating the standard of education in the profession. In 1836 he started the Southern
Medical and Surgical Journal, the first medical periodical published in
the South. It was by the faculty of the college which he was instru-
mental in founding, and through his pen, that the suggestion for holding a convention of the faculties of the medical colleges of the United
States, in 1836, was made. Although nothing was immediately accomplished, the discussion ripened into the movements which organized the
American Medical Association.*

The Willoughby University, Willoughby, Lake County, Ohio, was
chartered in 1834, and its first course of instruction commenced in 1835.
The medical department of the University of Louisiana, at New Orleans;
the Medical Institute of Geneva College, at Geneva, N. Y.; the medical
department of Cincinnati College, at Cincinnati, Ohio; and the Vermont
Medical School, at Woodstock, Vt., were chartered by the legislatures of
the respective States in which they were located, in the year 1835.

---

* See History of American Medical Association.

The medical department of the University of Louisville, Ky., was organized in 1837, and the medical department of the University of the City of New York the same year.

The medical department of Hampden Sidney College, at Richmond, Va., was organized in 1838. The Albany Medical College, at Albany, N. Y., and the medical department of the Pennsylvania College, at Philadelphia, in 1839. The Missouri Medical College, at St. Louis, was organized in 1840, and the St. Louis Medical College, in the same city, in 1841.

The legislature of the State of Illinois granted a charter for the Rush Medical College, in Chicago, in 1837, but a faculty was organized and the first course of instruction given in 1843. One of the principal founders of this school was the late Daniel Brainard, M. D., who held the chair of surgery in it until the time of his death, in 1866. The college building with most of its contents was totally destroyed by the great fire of 1871. The courses of instruction, however, were continued to good classes, and an elegant new college building was completed and occupied in the autumn of 1876.

The Cleveland Medical College was organized in Cleveland, Ohio, in 1843; the medical department of the University of Buffalo, in Buffalo, N. Y., in 1846; and the Starling Medical College and Hospital, at Columbus, Ohio, in 1847. The medical department of the University of Michigan, at Ann Arbor, was instituted in 1849. All the departments of the university are under the control of the State board of regents, and the professors are paid salaries from the public funds appropriated to that purpose, and consequently are not dependent on fees paid by students. The latter pay no annual tuition or lecture fees, but only an initiation fee on admission.

The medical department of the University of Nashville, at Nashville, Tenn., the College of Physicians and Surgeons, at Keokuk, Iowa, and the Woman's Medical College of Pennsylvania, at Philadelphia, were organized in 1850.

The Medical College of Virginia, at Richmond, the medical department of the University of Georgetown, at Washington, and the Cincinnati College of Medicine and Surgery, at Cincinnati, were created in 1851. The Savannah Medical College, at Savannah, Ga., and the Miami Medical College, at Cincinnati, were established in 1852.

The Atlanta Medical College was commenced at Atlanta, Ga., in 1855, and the Medical College of the Pacific, at San Francisco, in 1858.

The Chicago Medical College, medical department of the Northwestern University, at Chicago, was organized in 1859, and its first course of instruction was commenced in October of that year. It was first established as a department of Lind University of Chicago, an institution which had received a liberal charter from the legislature of the State of Illinois. It continued to be known as the Medical Department of Lind University until the spring of 1864, when, by mutual agreement between the medical faculty and the trustees of the university, the medical school became a separate and independent institution, organized under the general incorporation law of the State, and with the name changed to the Chicago Medical College. In 1869 it was adopted by the trustees of the Northwestern University as the medical department of that institution; it still, however, retaining its own charter and board of trustees.

The founders of this college, most of whom are still active members of its faculty, were actuated by a desire to place college medical instruction on a broader and more'systematic plan by lengthening the annual courses of instruction; by grading the students on the same principles as in other departments of learning, with the branches embraced in the curriculum divided into series corresponding with the grading of the classes; and requiring examinations at the close of each annual course, instead of deferring all examinations until the time for graduation. The college curriculum was made to embrace three courses of instruction, corresponding with the three years of study required, and designated junior, middle, and senior courses.

The junior course, designed for the first year of medical pupilage, was made to embrace descriptive anatomy, physiology and histology, materia medica, inorganic and practical chemistry, with dissections and training in the use of the microscope.

The middle course, designed for the second year of medical study, embraced general pathology and pathological anatomy, organic chemistry and toxicology, general therapeutics, surgical anatomy and operations of surgery, medical jurisprudence and hygiene, orthopedic surgery, psychological medicine, with hospital attendance.

The senior course, designed for the third year of medical study, embraced the principles and practice of medicine, principles and practice of surgery and military surgery, obstetrics and diseases of women and children, diseases of the eye and ear, hospital and dispensary attendance, daily, with individual training in auscultation and percussion, and in the use of all the instruments and appliances required for the diagnosis and treatment of diseases.

The full annual courses of instruction in these several departments were given between the first Monday in October and the third Tuesday in March following, the instruction to the three classes running parallel through the whole-term. Examinations were required and certificates of progress given at the end of the junior and middle courses, and a final examination for the degree of doctor of medicine at the end of the senior course.

In addition to the foregoing regular annual courses of instruction, a supplementary course was given each year, extending from the first Monday in April to the last Wednesday in June, devoted chiefly to clinical instruction in the hospital and dispensary, practical work in the laboratory, with didactic lectures on special topics.

The establishment of this school was the first attempt in this country to place medical college education upon a full graded and systematic plan, in accordance with the same principles that govern in all other branches of education. It also made actual attendance upon hospital clinical instruction, during at least one college term, one of the regular requirements for graduation. The plan thus adopted in the beginning has been continued to the present time, making such changes only as would render the system more complete in its practical working.

The school has had a regular healthy growth; its first classes for the term of 1859–'60 numbered 33, of whom 12 received the degree of M. D., and those for 1875–'76, numbered 148, of whom 53 graduated at the close of the term.

The Medical College of Mobile, Ala., and the Long Island College Hospital, in Brooklyn, N. Y., were organized in 1860; the Bellevue Hospital Medical College, in the city of New York, in 1861; and the Woman's Medical College of the New York Infirmary, located in the city of New York, in 1864. The medical department of the Willamette University, located at Salem, in Oregon Territory, was commenced in 1866; the medical department of Howard University, at Washington, D. C., in 1867; the medical department of the University of South Carolina, and the Detroit Medical College at Detroit, Mich., in 1868. The medical department of the University of Wooster, at Cleveland, Ohio; the Kansas City College of Physicians and Surgeons, at Kansas City, Mo.; the Louisville Medical College, at Louisville, Ky.;•the medical department of the Iowa State University, at Iowa City; and the medical department of the Indiana University, at Indianoplis, all had their beginning in 1869.

The Woman's Hospital Medical College, at Chicago, and the medical department of Lincoln University, at Oxford, Pa., were organized in 1870; and the Free Medical College for Women, in the city of New York, in 1871.

The Medical College of Evansville, Ind., chartered in 1846, was suspended for a time, and reorganized in 1872. The College of Physicians and Surgeons of the Syracuse University, at Syracuse, N. Y., and the College of Physicians and Surgeons, at Wilmington, N. C., were incorporated in 1872. The school at Syracuse adopted a graded system of college instruction similar to that of the Chicago Medical College. The medical department of the University of California, at San Francisco, was first organized under the name of the Toland Medical College, in 1864, and become a department of the University of California, in 1873.

The medical department of the University of the State of Missouri, at Columbia, Mo., and the Texas Medical College and Hospital at Galveston, Tex., were organized in 1873.

Medical schools have recently been established in Portland, Me., and in Baltimore, Md., the exact dates of the formation of which are not at hand.

STATISTICAL RÉSUMÉ.

From the foregoing statistics we learn that during the thirty years intervening between the close of the war for independence and 1810, seven medical schools were organized; in the thirty years intervening between 1810 and 1840, twenty-six new medical colleges were added to the list; and in the thirty-five years since 1840 the number of new medical schools created is forty-seven; making the whole number of medical educational institutions established in the United States during the first century of our history as a nation, eighty. We have not included in these numbers five or six mere abortive attempts to form medical schools in different localities, institutions so transient as to leave a record difficult to trace. Of the eighty which have been established, sixteen have been discontinued or suspended, leaving at this date, 1876, sixty-four medical colleges in active operation in our country.

Of these, Maine has two; New Hampshire, one; Vermont, three; Massachusetts, one; Connecticut, one; New York, nine; Pennsylvania, four; Maryland, three; Virginia, two; South Carolina, one; Georgia, three; Alabama, one; Louisiana, two; Texas, one; Tennessee, one; Kentucky, three; Missouri, three; California, two; Oregon, one; Iowa, two; Illinois, three; Indiana, three; Ohio, seven; Michigan, two; and the District of Columbia, three; leaving thirteen States without any medical college now in operation.

Four of the colleges included in the foregoing enumeration are devoted exclusively to the education of women in medicine; namely, two in New York City, one in Philadelphia, and one in Chicago.

The whole number of students attending the medical colleges in 1810 was about 650, of whom about 100 graduated at the close of the college terms for that year. The population of the United States at that time was 7,239,881. In 1840 the whole number of students in the medical colleges was about 2,500, of whom about 800 received the degree of doctor of medicine. The population of the United States in that year was 17,069,453. During the college terms of 1875–'76 the whole number of medical students in attendance on the colleges was 6,650, of whom 2,200 received the degree of doctor of medicine. The population of the States at the same time was over 40,000,000.

Without claiming absolute accuracy for the foregoing figures, they are sufficiently close for all the purposes of comparison. And they show clearly, notwithstanding all that has been said about the rapid multiplication of medical schools, that the colleges and the students during the last thirty-five years have increased in a ratio only about equal to the ratio of increase in the population of the country. The whole number engaged in teaching as professors in the several medical colleges at this time is about five hundred. In the foregoing statistics are not included colleges or schools for teaching exclusively dentistry,

pharmacy, and exclusive dogmas in medicine. Of the first there are
eleven; of the second, thirteen; of the third, eleven, three of which are
called eclectic and eight homœopathic.

CHARACTER AND PURPOSES OF EARLY MEDICAL SCHOOLS.

The reader of the foregoing pages will readily see that the origin of
medical schools in this country has been solely from individual efforts,
put forth from time to time, as the ambition of the individual or the
supposed wants of the country demanded, and not from any well
digested scheme or official plan of professional education adopted either
by the States or by the General Government.

This remark is true, not only in relation to the origin of medical
schools, but equally so in regard to their continuance and multiplication
to the present time. Whenever the legislature of any State has been
asked to grant a charter for a medical college, the request has generally
been complied with ; and in the few instances in which such requests
have been denied, the parties interested have seldom found difficulty in
forming a connection with some literary college or university already
having authority to confer degrees in medicine as well as in general
science. Some of the State legislatures, in addition to liberally granting charters for medical colleges, have also occasionally appropriated a
few thousand dollars to aid in the erection of suitable buildings, but
rarely to endow professorships or to defray any of the current expenses
of such institutions. In the University of Michigan, and possibly in
one or two other State universities, the medical professorships, like
those of the other departments, are sustained by the income from the
general endowment, independent of the fees paid by medical students.
We may say in general terms, therefore, that the whole system of medical education in this country, represented to-day by sixty-four medical
colleges distributed among twenty-four separate States, sustained by
the active work of over five hundred professors, and annually aiding
in the professional education of nearly seven thousand students, is the
spontaneous outgrowth of the profession itself—self reliant, and almost
wholly self sustained. Originating among a free people, under the laws
of various educationally independent States, apparently striving to keep
pace in the increase of their number and efficiency with a population
which, in one century, has increased from three millions to forty millions, and extended over a territory from the Atlantic to the Pacific
and from the St. Lawrence to the Gulf of Mexico, under circumstances
of the freest competition, these schools constitute a subject worthy of
the most careful study.

We have already seen that our medical colleges had their origin at a
time when medical science and art occupied a far narrower field than
at present—a time when obstetrics was yet chiefly in the hands of un-
lettered midwives ; surgery an appendage to anatomy ; and organic

chemistry, histology, and even physiology, as now recognized, hardly known ; a time, too, when it was the universal practice for regular students of medicine to apprentice themselves to private preceptors of reputation, from whom they expected to receive the greater part of their professional education.

The great and pressing need, at that time, was for schools in which, after gaining a knowledge of the text books, the rude pharmacy of the preceptor's office, and the individual experience of the preceptor him- self, during the first two or three years of his study, the student could review the whole in connection with such experimental demonstrations as could be given only in the laboratory, the dissecting room, and the clinical wards of the public hospital. The idea of the college was to supplement, not supersede, the work of the private preceptor.

Precisely this was what the medical colleges were originally adjusted to do, and they fulfilled the object well. Although originating in dif- ferent States, wholly independent of each other, and in direct rivalry for patronage, on which they depended for support, they were remark- ably similar in their organization and requirements. At first the num- ber of professors in each school was small, and the college term eight or nine months ; offering the bachelor's degree after three years of study and one college term, and the doctor's degree after one or two more years and a second course of college attendance. But as most of the students lived in small towns and country districts, remote from the colleges, making attendance on the lectures both tedious and expensive, only a part of those engaged in the study of medicine ever reached a medical college, and most of those, after taking the bachelor's degree, never returned to take a second course and the higher degree of doctor. These circumstances constituted a strong inducement for the colleges to concentrate the annual period of instruction into as short a time as possible, both for the purpose of increasing the number of stu- dents who could afford the means of attending, and the number who would take the second degree.

Under these influences, the first thirty years sufficed to cause the bachelor's degree to be abandoned by all the schools, the number of professors in each school to be doubled, and the length of the annual college term to be shortened one-third. And in twenty-five years more, from the same causes, aided efficiently by the fact that the degrees con- ferred by the colleges became practically recognized throughout the whole country as a sufficient license to practise medicine in all its de- partments, the colleges, with only one exception worth noting, had each from five to seven professorships occupied by as many different profess- ors, and annual college terms of twelve to sixteen weeks, during which the students in one class listened to five or six didactic lectures a day, on as many different subjects, besides attending to dissections and clini- cal instruction when such were accessible.

The requirements for the degree of doctor of medicine were three years of study with some regular practitioner of medicine, including attendance on two courses of college instruction, such as just described, the one being simply a repetition of the other; the writing of a thesis on some medical subject; the possession of a good moral character; the attainment of twenty-one years of age; and the sustaining of a creditable examination in the several branches of medicine at the close of the second course of lectures.

It will be seen that in these requirements there was no reference to any standard of preliminary education to be attained by the student before entering upon his professional studies, except the ability to write a thesis. The requirement of a knowledge of Greek and Latin and the writing of a thesis in the Latin language was abandoned on the full reorganization of the University of Pennsylvania, in 1792. The relinquishment of natural philosophy, natural history, and botany, as requirements, soon followed, leaving only the single indirect trace of any non-professional education to which we have alluded.

Under these conditions and tendencies, by the end of the second thirty years of our history the number of medical colleges had increased from five to forty-one; the number of students attending them, from six hundred and fifty to twenty-five hundred; and the ratio of those graduating each year, from less than one in six to one in three.

CHANGES AND RESULTS.

Here we see a system of medical colleges originating spontaneously to supply the wants of a free and rapidly increasing people, and open to the most unrestricted rivalry, actively developing two apparently opposite results. In one direction the schools properly vie with each other in increasing the number of their professors, in full consonance with the rapid advancement of the medical sciences; they sagaciously seek out and enlist the services, as teachers, of the most learned, eloquent, and industrious men to be found in the profession; they spend time and money freely in filling laboratories, anatomical rooms, and museums with all the means for efficient teaching and illustration. So far their free rivalry has reference only to their office as teaching bodies, institutions for imparting instruction, and is productive of nothing but good to the profession and the people. But the anomaly consists in the fact that, at the same time they were increasing their professors, the same institutions were rapidly shortening their annual courses; cutting off all collateral requirements; failing to grade the branches of medical study as they increased in number and extent, so as to adapt them to the several years of pupilage; and even reducing the final examination to the simple process of asking a few oral questions in the mysterious " greenroom."

This most unfortunate tendency of our experiment in permitting the freest rivalry in the establishment of medical schools, results directly and necessarily from the fact that the degrees they confer, and the diplomas they give, have been permitted throughout the whole country, with only a few temporary exceptions, to have all the force and effect of a license to practise medicine. It requires but a moderate familiarity with the motives that govern human actions to see clearly that in a country where there are no entailments of estates, and where the great body of young men who seek the professions are without pecuniary fortunes, and largely dependent on their own industry for the means of education as well as reputation and fortune in after life, the question "Where can I get the degree of doctor, which is equivalent to a license to practise and a full admission into the ranks of the medical profession in the shortest time and consequently with the least expenditure of time and money?" exerts a very great if not controlling influence in determining where the student shall attend his college instruction. Not that medical students are a whit less conscientious in their desire to fully qualify themselves for the responsible duties of our profession than those who seek any other calling in life; but present necessity, or even convenience, easily controls when there comes with it the flattering thought that, at another time, after having earned a little money by practice, all deficiencies can be supplied by a season of reviewing in a school of the largest facilities.

Just on this half unconscious delusion, hundreds are induced to go where the requirements in time and money are least, regardless of all other advantages. The medical college in a country village, remote from all facilities for clinical instruction in hospital or dispensary, and but scantily supplied with subjects for dissection, can issue to its graduates just as large a diploma, couched in just as unintelligible Latin, and having much the same influence with the people as the school in a metropolitan city whose students can have the largest facilities for clinical and practical study. Hence it is not strange that, before the end of the seventh decade of the past century of our existence as a nation, about forty medical colleges had been organized, only sixteen of which were so situated as to afford their students any proper facilities for clinical instruction; and that those sixteen were resorted to by a little more than one-third of the whole number of those who attended medical colleges.

The general acceptance of the college diploma as full admission into the profession, thereby uniting in the hands of the same men the business of teaching and the power of licensing, has continued to the present day. It is wholly responsible for the fact that, while we have sixty-four medical colleges to-day, one-third of them are so located that they can afford their students no advantages for clinical instruction worthy of mention; and all except three or four still attempt to crowd instruction in all the departments of medicine upon the attention of mixed or ungraded classes, in annual college terms of from sixteen to twenty weeks, and exact only two such strictly repetitional courses for graduation.

This state of things, in regard to our medical schools, is made still worse by the fact that, during the century under consideration, the system of private medical pupilage has undergone a complete change. At the beginning of that period, as we have already seen, the private study under a master was a protracted and serious work, and the resort to the college was simply to review and more fully illustrate that work; but steadily, as medical colleges increased in number, as population became more dense, and as steamboats and railroads increased a thousandfold the facilities for travel, the work of private pupilage relaxed. Indentures of medical students, as pupils, to the more noted practitioners long since ceased, and the relations of student and preceptor have become merely nominal in practice; in nine cases out of ten consisting in little more than the registry of the student's name in the doctor's office, permission to read the books of his library or not, as he chooses, and the giving of a certificate of time of study for the student to take to the medical college where he expects to graduate.

The relative positions of private pupilage and collegiate study have undergone a complete practical reversal. The latter, instead of reviewing and supplementing the former, has become the student's chief reliance for the acquisition of medical knowledge; and hence, to have maintained its adaptation or adjustment to the needs of the profession, it should have not only increased the number of its professors and its means for communicating knowledge, but also the length of its annual courses, and the division or gradation of its classes in accordance with their period of study, and in proportion to the greatly enlarged field of medical knowledge to be acquired.

Such would have been to-day the grand result worked out by our experiment of self originating and self sustaining medical schools, had they been restricted to their only appropriate functions as institutions for imparting medical instruction and advancing medical science, instead of being hampered and perverted from their natural course by assuming the office of licensing institutions; and if this incubus could be removed to-day another quarter of a century would not pass before every medical college in our country would have its annual course of instruction extended to six months, its curriculum and classes so graded that the attention of each student should be restricted to the branches adapted to his period of advancement in study, and nine-tenths of all our medical students would be in attendance on those colleges only which should afford proper facilities for full clinical and demonstrative instruction.

Let the only question presented to the mind of the student, when choosing the college he shall attend, be, where can he most certainly obtain that amount and variety of medical knowledge which will enable him successfully to pass the examination of an independent board of examiners, acting under liberal and proper rules and modes of testing the student's knowledge, and we shall have nothing to fear either from the number or the rivalry of our medical schools.

THE EVIL OF UNITING TEACHING AND LICENSING AND ITS REFORM.

The injurious tendencies of our system of uniting the work of teaching and that of licensing to practice, in an unlimited number of independent medical colleges, were seen at an early period, and clearly pointed out; and by none more clearly than by some of those engaged as teachers themselves. So true is this that the legislatures of some of the States, in organizing and regulating their respective State medical societies, made some ineffectual attempts to lessen the evil by legislation. This was more particularly the case in South Carolina, Maryland, Delaware, Massachusetts, and New York.

As early as 1839, at an annual meeting of the Medical Society of the State of New York, the following resolution was adopted by a vote of fourteen to four:

Resolved, That the right of teaching ought to be separated as much as possible from the power of conferring degrees or license.

The following year a committee, consisting of James R. Manly, M. D., of New York City; T. Romeyn Beck, M. D., of Albany; and John McCall M. D., of Utica, submitted to the same society an able and interesting report on the subject of medical education, in which occurs the following pertinent and significant language:

But in view of the diploma becoming depreciated by the rapid establishment of new schools, it may well become a question deserving serious consideration whether, at no distant period, the right of teaching and licensing should not be *disjoined.* An incidental difficulty to the adoption of this suggestion is the fact that we are surrounded by institutions in other States which might or might not follow it, and thus our students be induced to desert our own colleges.[*]

In 1837 the same view was advocated by some of the ablest members of the profession in Philadelphia, and they proceeded so far as to organize an institution for the purpose of examining candidates and of conferring degrees wholly independent of the business of teaching. A petition signed by one hundred and twenty-six physicians, residents of that city, was presented to the legislature of the State, asking for a charter giving legal effect to their organization, but the charter was not granted, and the project failed.

In 1844 the subject was again brought prominently under consideration in the New York State Medical Society by the writer of these pages. The discussion of the same subject was continued in the annual meeting of 1855, and resulted in the call issued by that society for a convention of delegates from all the medical colleges and societies in the United States, which was held in New York, in May, 1846, and from which originated the American Medical Association.

We make these historical allusions to show that neither those engaged in medical teaching, nor the profession at large, have been unmindful of the evil to which so much importance has been attached.

---

[*] See Transactions of the New York State Medical Society for 1840.

Yet it still exists in all its force. That the colleges have failed to keep themselves adjusted to the needs of the profession, in regard to the length of their annual courses of instruction, the systematic classification of the branches included in their curricula, the corresponding grading or division of their classes, and the exaction of a reasonable standard of preliminary education, has been still more fully appreciated and acknowledged. Not only is this appreciation indicated by the criticisms in our medical periodicals and the discussions in our medical societies—and by the more general efforts of the colleges, since 1850, to increase the number of their professors, the fulness of their curricula, and the piecing out of their annual courses of instruction by two or three weeks of preliminary lecturing at the beginning and short spring courses at the end of the regular terms, all of which the student might attend or not as he chose—but, in a still more formal manner, by the proceedings of two or three conventions of delegates from the schools only, in which all the defects here stated relating to preliminary education, inadequate length of the annual courses of instruction, and the urgent need of a systematic division of the branches taught into groups appropriate for each year of study, and the consequent grading of the classes, with annual examinations of each class, have been fully stated, and a thorough plan for remedying them devised and urgently recommended to the schools for their adoption.

The first of the conventions to which we allude was held in Cincinnati, in May, 1867, and was presided over by the learned president of the medical faculty of the University of Pennsylvania. The second was held in the city of Washington, in May, 1870, and was presided over by the justly distinguished head of the faculty of the Jefferson Medical College. A third convention of less formal character was held in the city of Chicago, in June, 1876. If you ask me why these reasonable and highly important recommendations have not been adopted by the majority of the schools, I can only point you for answer to the paragraph already quoted from the report on medical education made to the New York State Medical Society, in 1840, by that learned trio, composed of Beck, Manley, and McCall ; or, more directly, to the fact that while the faculty of each school frankly acknowledges the defects in adaptation to the present enlarged field of medical science and art, and the urgent needs of the profession, each waits for the other to move first, lest by placing higher requirements upon the time and resources of the student it should cause its own halls to be deserted for those of its less exacting neighbor.

The efforts in this direction, however, have not been entirely fruitless of practical results. In 1859 the Chicago Medical College, now the medical department of the Northwestern University, was organized for the express purpose of testing the practicability of establishing a school with a thoroughly graded and consecutive system of instruction. Its curriculum was made to embrace thirteen professorships, arranged in three groups, one appropriate for each of the three years of study required. The students attending were correspondingly divided into three classes, junior, middle, and senior. Each class was required to devote its time thoroughly to the group of branches and lectures belonging to its year of advancement in study, and to be examined fully in those branches at the end of the college term. Each of the three courses was continued six months of the year, and actual attendance on hospital clinical instruction and practical work in the chemical, anatomical, and microscopic or histological laboratories was added to the requisites for eligibility to graduation. The very satisfactory success of this institution during the past fifteen years and its present prosperity certainly demonstrate the practicability of the scheme.

In 1871 the medical school of Harvard University, one of the oldest and most influential medical institutions in our country, also adopted a fully graded system of instruction, dividing her classes, and extending her courses of instruction throughout the collegiate year, and has continued this plan to the present time, adding annually to the perfection of its details, and adding also to her own prosperity and influence. The new medical school of Syracuse University, New York, has practically adopted the same scheme; and the annual announcements of several other medical schools, for the present year, including some of the most influential and important institutions in the country, give unmistakable evidence of their having taken initial steps in the direction of this most desirable change.

But our medical schools, aided by the work of the private preceptor do not constitute the whole educational force or influence operating upon the profession in this country. Our social or society organizations, city, county, district, State, and national, have exerted throughout the whole period of our history a most potent influence over the educational interests of the profession.

II.—SOCIAL MEDICAL ORGANIZATIONS.

No apology is necessary for including medical societies among the educational institutions of our profession; for whatever increases the enterprise, stimulates the spirit of philosophical investigation, or adds an item to the stock of knowledge possessed by the profession, or whatever elevates it in the scale of social existence, is as truly a part of its educational means as is the study of its text books and the frequenting of its schools. The latter may, indeed, constitute the foundation, but many other things are required to complete the superstructure of a fair medical education.

And among these other things, no one is of greater importance than well organized associations, admitting of frequent communication and free interchange of thought among their members. Such associations not only elicit observations, stimulate investigations, and save from oblivion numberless facts; but they counteract the selfish feelings of individuality, they diffuse knowledge, they elevate the social feelings, and they embody and generalize facts that would otherwise remain isolated and useless.

The organization of the New Jersey State Medical Society in 1766, and that of Delaware in 1776, has already been mentioned in the first part of this report. The next important step in this direction was the passage of an act by the legislature of Massachusetts in 1781, incorporating the Massachusetts Medical Society. The objects set forth in the act of incorporatio n were the promotion of medical science and the regulation of all matters pertaini ng to the profession. To enable it to accomplish these desirable objects, the society was authorized to appoint a board of censors, whose duty it was to examine all candidates for admission into the profession in that State, and grant licenses to such as were found qualified. This society, together with that formed in New Haven in 1784, and the New Hampshire Society, chartered in 1791, exerted a very sal utary influence over the profession throughout the Eastern States.* To encourage the cultivation of individual talent and still further promote the advancement of medical science, a wealthy and enlightened citizen of Boston, Mr. Ward Nicholas Boylston, established in 1798 a perpetual legacy, yielding $133 per annum. Thirty-three dollars of this sum were to aid in the establishment of an anatomical museum, and the remaining one hundred to be awarded annually as premi ums for medical essays, under the direction of the fellows of the Massachusetts Medical Society. The noble intentions of the donor have been faithfully carried out by the society, thereby calling into existence annually a number of interesting essays which now embrace many of the most important topics belonging to medical science.

The Massachusetts Medical Society also enjoys the honor of being the first in this country to issue a regular volume of transactions, filled with the most interesting papers read before it. The first number of the transactions was published previous to 1800, and contained papers written by E. A. Holyoke, M. D., of Salem; William Baylies, M. D., of Dighton; Joseph Orne, M. D., of Salem; N. W. Appleton, M. D., of Boston; Edward A. Wyer, M. D., of Halifax, N. S.; Isaac Rand, M. D., of Cambridge; Isaac Rand, jr., M. D., of Boston; Joseph Osgood, M. D., of Andover; Thomas Welsh, M. D., of Boston; and Thomas Kast, M. D., of Boston.

The most important of these papers were: "An account of the weather and epidemics of Salem, in the county of Essex, for the year 1786, with a bill of mortality for the same year," by E. A. Holyoke, M. D., written in 1787; "A case of empyema successfully treated by an operation," by Isaac Rand, M. D., 1783; "Observations on hydro-

---

* Since writing the above, I learn from a reliable source that the Connecticut Medical Society, organized in New Haven in 1784, published a volume of transactions in 1788.

cephalus internus, by operation," by Isaac Rand, jr., in 1789; and "An account of an aneurism of the thigh perfectly cured by an operation, and the use of the limb preserved," by Thomas Kast, in 1790. The second volume of the society's transactions was not published until 1808.

The Philadelphia College of Physicians was formed in 1787 and incorporated by an act of the legislature of Pennsylvania in 1789. The Philadelphia Medical Society was organized in the same city in 1789, and was incorporated in 1792. A brief history of the last named society may be found in the Medical News and Library for January, 1843.

The medical society which had existed in New Jersey since 1766 was incorporated by an act of the legislature in 1790, under the name of the Medical Society of the State of New Jersey. The act of incorporation conferred the power to appoint censors for the purpose of examining and licensing candidates for permission to practise in that State; also to establish district or county societies, whose delegates were to constitute the parent or State society. The term of study required and all the regulations adopted were similar to those prescribed by the law of 1760 in New York.

The Medical Society of South Carolina was organized in 1789 and incorporated in 1794, but the provision for examining and licensing candidates for admission into the profession was made in 1817.

In 1799 the Medical and Chirurgical Faculty of the State of Maryland was incorporated, with power to elect, " by ballot, twelve persons of the greatest medical and chirurgical abilities in the State, who shall be styled the Medical Board of Examiners for the State of Maryland." It was the duty of this board " to grant licenses to such medical and chirurgical gentlemen as they, either upon a full examination or upon the production of diplomas from some respectable college, may judge adequate to commence the practice of the medical and chirurgical arts." Under a supplementary act passed in 1801 the board of examiners required all graduates of medical colleges, as well as others, to apply for and obtain a license before being authorized to practise. The penalty for violating these provisions was $50 for each offence, to be recovered in the county court where the offender may reside; and the judges of those courts were directed to present the several acts relating to medicine and surgery, annually, in charge to their respective grand juries.* Every person licensed by the examining board was, by virtue of such license, constituted a member of the State society. It is thus seen that Maryland was not only among the earliest to enact laws to protect her citizens against the inroads of ignorance and empiricism, but also that her laws relating to this subject were both simple and effectual.

The law for organizing State and county medical societies in New York was passed by the legislature of that State in April, 1806. The

---

* See act of incorporation, supplementary acts, &c. 18mo. Baltimore, 1822.

character of the law and its sanction by the governor were chiefly due to the enlightened views and labors of John Stearns, M. D., Alexander Sheldon, M. D., and Asa Fitch, M. D., who, as a committee, represented the profession in the counties of Saratoga, Montgomery, and Washington. The first two were members of the legislature at that time, and were greatly aided in the final passage of the bill by Hon. William W. Van Ness. The law authorized the legally qualified physicians and surgeons of each county to form themselves into a society, named after the county in which it was formed, with power to choose officers, make all needful rules for the government of its members, and appoint a board of censors to examine and license all the applicants for admission into the profession in their respective counties; but no one could be admitted to an examination until he had given evidence of having studied three years with some practitioner, and had arrived at the age of twenty-one years. A State medical society was also provided for, to be composed of one delegate from each county society, and such permanent members as the society should from time to time elect, not exceeding two in any one year. It was required to meet annually, at the capitol in the city of Albany, to elect officers and to transact such other business as the interests of the profession should require. It was also required to divide the State into four medical districts, and to appoint a board of censors for each, whose duty it was to examine all candidates for license to practise medicine and surgery who should present themselves, after having studied the required length of time. The law also forbade any one to enter upon the practice of medicine and collect pay for his services without first procuring either a license from a county or State society or a diploma from some regularly organized medical college. Candidates who might be rejected by a county board had the right to appeal to the censors of the State society for another examination; but not vice versa. Within two years after the passage of this law nearly every county in the State had a regularly organized medical society with its board of censors and the commencement of a library.

The first meeting of the State society was held at the capitol in Albany, in February, 1807; its organization was completed according to the provisions of the law. Thus two great and important objects were accomplished, namely, a thorough organization of the profession in a manner most favorable for its advancement in science and social elevation, and the provision for having all candidates examined before admission by practitioners themselves, without the intervention of any other class.

In the same year, 1807, an act was passed making some further provisions relating to the internal organization of the State society, and also prescribing a penalty of $5 a month for practising without being authorized according to the act of the previous year. This penalty, however, was not to apply to persons using, for the benefit of the sick, any roots or herbs the growth of the United States.

In May, 1812, the legislature increased the foregoing penalty to $25 for each offence, and required that all licenses in future should be deposited in the county clerk's office. The proviso exempting from penalty those who might use, for the sick, such roots or herbs as are the growth of the United States, though evidently designed only to protect nurses and families in the use of simple domestic remedies yet served the purpose of covering all kinds of quackery, it being only necessary to plead the use of nothing but indigenous remedies.

In 1813 the several preceding acts were revised and consolidated into one statute, and continued without alteration until 1818, when the legislature passed an act increasing the term of medical study to four years; but one year might be deducted if the student had pursued classical studies that length of time, after the age of sixteen years, or had attended a complete course of the lectures delivered by each of the professors in some regular medical college.

In the following year another act was passed prohibiting the medical colleges from granting the degree of doctor of medicine to any student who had not fully complied with the requirements of the law of 1818.

The next law of importance enacted in New York was passed by the legislature in 1827. This leaves the term of study and the conditions for obtaining a license or a diploma essentially the same as before, but the twelfth section provides that—

No person shall receive from the regents of the university of the State a diploma conferring the degree of doctor of medicine unless he shall have pursued the study of medical science for at least three years after the age of sixteen with some physician or surgeon duly authorized by law to practise his profession, and shall also have attended two complete courses of all the lectures delivered in an incorporated medical college, and have attended the last of such courses in the college by which he shall be recommended for his degree.

And section twentieth declares that no person under the age of twenty-one years can be entitled to practise physic and surgery in that State. Another provision of this law required all regularly licensed physicians to file a copy of their license or diploma in the clerk's office, and become members of the county society in the county of their residence before they were legally entitled to collect pay for their services.

The foregoing provisions and penalties continued on the statute books, though seldom enforced against unlicensed practitioners, until 1843, when the penalty for practising without a license and the prohibition of power to collect fees were both repealed, but leaving the provisions regulating medical education and organization of medical societies unchanged.

The laws of New Jersey were so amended in 1816 as to prohibit all unlicensed persons who were not already engaged in practice from entering upon those duties in that State, under a penalty of $25 for each offence. Such persons were also disqualified from collecting any compensation for their services. And instead of containing the neutralizing proviso which we have noticed in the laws of 1813 and 1818, in New York, the New Jersey law declared that—

This act shall be so construed as to prevent all irregular bred pretenders to the healing art, under the names or titles of practical botanists, root or Indian doctors, or any other name or title involving quackery of any species, from practising their deceptions, and imposing on the ignorance and credulity of their fellow citizens.

Some unimportant alterations in the medical laws of New Jersey were made by the legislature in the years 1818, 1823, 1825, 1830, 1838, but without changing essentially their more important provisions.

The Rhode Island State Medical Society was incorporated in 1812, and that of Maine in 1821. The regulations adopted in all the New England States were very similar. They all required the appointment of State or district boards of censors for examining and licensing candidates to practise; also some degree of preliminary education, a term of medical study not less than three years, and the attainment of twenty-one years of age. In Massachusetts, Rhode Island, and New Hampshire, the boards of censors were unconnected with the medical colleges of those States; and the laws required all persons intending to commence practice, whether educated in those States or already licensed by the institutions of other States, to apply to some one of the boards of censors for a license before they were authorized to enforce payment for their services. In Connecticut and Maine but one board of censors was established in each State, which was authorized to examine all candidates, whether for a license or the higher degree of doctor of medicine. These boards were composed, in the one State, of the medical faculty of Yale College, associated with an equal number of censors appointed by the president and fellows of the Connecticut State Medical Society, the president of the society being always one of the number; and, in the other, of the medical faculty of Bowdoin College, and an equal number of censors chosen by the Maine State Medical Society.

In 1822 the legislature of the State of Delaware passed a law enabling the medical society of that State to appoint a board of medical examiners consisting of fifteen members, whose term of office was to continue five years, and who were directed to examine and license all candidates found qualified to practise in that State. The requisites for admission to an examination by such board were three years' study with some respectable practitioner, the attendance on one full course of lectures in some medical college, and the attainment of twenty-one years of age; but graduates of respectable colleges were licensed, on the exhibition of their diplomas, without an examination. The same penalties were enacted against unlicensed practitioners as in the State of Maryland.

The Medical Society of the District of Columbia was incorporated by an act of Congress in 1819, with power to appoint a board of censors, composed of five practitioners, whose duties and privileges were the same as those appointed by the Delaware State Medical Society; and the same penalty was enacted against unlicensed and irregular practitioners.

The States of South Carolina, Georgia, Alabama, Mississippi, and Louisiana have all had laws of a similar character for the regulation of medical education and practice.

In 1817 the legislature of South Carolina enacted a law providing for the establishment of two medical boards of examiners, one in Charleston and the other in Columbia. They were required to examine all applicants for permission to practise in that State, except such as had received a diploma from some medical college, and to grant licenses to those they deemed qualified; and every person practising without such license or diploma was liable to be indicted and fined in a sum not exceeding $500, and imprisoned a term not exceeding two months. These regulations continued in force until 1838, when all restrictions and penalties were abolished by an act of the legislature. The act by which a fine of $500 was provided for all persons who should practise physic in Georgia without a license from the board of physicians was passed in 1826, and continued in force until 1835, when it was repealed. In 1839 the examining board of physicians was reorganized and again invested with power to examine applicants and grant licenses, but with the following proviso, which practically nullified the whole act:

Provided nothing in the said revised act shall be so construed as to operate against the Thomsonian or botanic practice, or any other practitioner of medicine in this State.

In Alabama an act was passed in December, 1823, requiring the establishment of five boards of medical examiners in the State, each consisting of three members, elected by a joint vote of both houses of the State legislature. Their powers and duties, in regard to examining and licensing candidates for admission into the profession, were the same as those existing in South Carolina. The penalty for practising without a license or diploma was a sum not exceeding $500 for each offence. But the examining boards were all abolished between 1840 and 1845, which operated as a repeal of all laws on the subject.

In Mississippi, laws regulating the practice of medicine very similar to those in South Carolina and Alabama were enacted by the first legislature after the organization of the State government. The Medical Society of the State of Mississippi was organized in accordance with a law passed by the legislature in 1829. The laws of this State establishing boards of examiners, registering licenses, organizing the State society, and prohibiting all irregular practice were very complete and efficient. But when the State constitution was revised, in 1834, the several boards of examiners were omitted, which operated as a repeal of all restraints on the practice of medicine in that State. The State medical society, however, continued its organization, though with less efficiency, for many years later.

In Louisiana, laws relating to the practice of physic and surgery were passed in 1808 and revised in 1816 and 1820. In the latter year two medical boards were established, one for each supreme judicial district in the State, each to consist of six members, with one apothecary attached to the board in the first district; and all to be appointed by the governor, with the advice and consent of the senate. It was the duty of these boards to examine all candidates for license to practise in their respective districts, and license such as were found qualified; but those who had graduated at some respectable medical college were permitted to obtain a license, on exhibiting their diploma, without an examination. The apothecary attached to the board in the first district was to examine and license apothecaries, who were under the same regulations as practising physicians. The penalties for violating the laws of this State, by practising without a license, were a fine of $100 for. the first offence, and, for the second, a fine not exceeding $200 and imprisonment not more than one year. The attorney-general was required to prosecute for all violations of the law. No legal provision was made for organizing a State medical society.

The Tennessee State Medical Society was incorporated by an act of the legislature in 1830, with a board of censors authorized to examine and license all persons who might present themselves for examination touching their skill in the practice of medicine and surgery; but no term of study was required, and no penalties were provided for practising without a license.

In Ohio, Indiana, and Michigan, laws were passed, soon after the respective State governments were organized, incorporating State, county, or district medical societies, with power to appoint censors and license candidates to practise, very similar to the laws relating to the same subjects in New York.

From the foregoing brief reference to medical legislation, and the organization of medical societies, it will be seen that during the first thirty or forty years of our national history the legislatures of nearly all the States then existing, except Pennsylvania, Virginia, and North Carolina, had enacted laws for the avowed purpose of protecting the citizens from the impositions of ignorance and empiricism, and of promoting medical science. That these were the real motives for enacting the laws referred to, and especially the first one named, that of protecting the citizen against imposition, is abundantly shown by the preambles and titles attached to the several acts. The idea of protecting the profession, or of investing it with special privileges, was the discovery of a later period, and was diligently fostered by all the advocates of the various *pathies* and *isms*. of the day. And yet so persistently did the advocates of these represent to the politicians and legislators of that time the idea that all the penalties and restrictions against uneducated and unlicensed practitioners were only designed to enable the regular profession to enjoy a monopoly of the practice, and to restrict the liberty of the citizen in the employment of whomsoever he pleased, that during the decade from 1840 to 1850 nearly all such restrictions and penalties were repealed by the legislatures of the several States. This, together with the rapid increase in the number of medical colleges, and the much larger proportion of students who obtained diplomas instead of applying to the examining boards for license, caused such boards to become neglected and practically useless, and even many of the State medical societies ceased to maintain an active existence.

It was during this period of adverse legislation and active aggression on the part of the advocates of the two leading systems of exclusive dogmas in medicine that the movement in favor of establishing a permanent national medical organization began to attract attention and to assume definite shape. The first distinct proposition for a national convention emanated from the faculty of the Medical College of Georgia, at Augusta, and was advocated in the columns of the Southern Medical and Surgical Journal, published at the same place, as early as 1835. The proposition was limited, however, to a call for delegates from medical colleges only, and was sustained by those desiring an extension of the lecture term in the colleges and a higher standard of attainments for graduation. Although the project elicited considerable discussion, no action was taken concerning it by some of the older and more influential schools, and consequently no convention was held. The topics involved, nevertheless, continued to be discussed in the medical periodicals, and still more freely in the anniversary meetings of the State and district medical societies. At the annual meeting of the Medical Society of the State of New York, in February, 1839, John McCall, M. D., of Utica, offered the following preamble and resolution, which were adopted by the society:

Whereas a national medical convention would advance, in the apprehension of this society, the cause of the medical profession throughout our land, in thus affording an interchange of views and sentiments on the most interesting of all subjects, that involving men's health, and the means of securing or recovering the same: Therefore,

Resolved, That in our opinion such convention is deemed advisable and important, and we would hence recommend that it be held in the year 1840, on the first Tuesday in May of that year, in the city of Philadelphia, and that it consist of three delegates from each State medical society and one from each regularly constituted medical school in the United States; and that the president and secretary of this society be and they are hereby instructed and required to transmit, as soon as may be, a circular to that effect to each State medical society and medical school in the United States.

This proposition was approved by several State medical societies, and delegates were appointed by some of them, but the societies and schools in Philadelphia did not respond, and no convention was held. The subject of medical education, however, continued to elicit discussion at nearly every meeting of medical societies in all parts of the country. Some resolutions were presented to the New York State Medical Society at its annual meeting in February, 1844, by the writer of these pages, then a young member representing the Broome County society, and by Alexander Thompson, M. D., of Cayuga County, both advocating a higher standard of attainments for students of medicine, and the withdrawal of the licensing authority from the colleges. These resolutions led to much discussion, which was renewed at the next annual meeting, in 1845, and resulted in the adoption of the following preamble and resolutions, offered by the present writer:*

Whereas it is believed that a national medical convention would be conducive to the elevation of the standard of medical education in the United States; and whereas there is no mode of accomplishing so desirable an object without concert of action on the part of the medical colleges, societies, and institutions of all the States: Therefore,

Resolved, That the New York State Medical Society earnestly recommends a national convention of delegates from medical societies and colleges in the whole Union, to con-vene in the city of New York on the first Tuesday in May, in the year 1846, for the purpose of adopting some concerted action on the subject set forth in the foregoing preamble.

Resolved, That a committee of three be appointed to carry the foregoing resolution into effect. †

The committee appointed in compliance with the last resolution consisted of N. S. Davis, M. D., of Binghamton, and James McNaughton, M. D., and Peter Van Buren, M. D., of Albany. The committee discharged its duties faithfully and successfully, and the proposed convention was held at the time appointed, May, 1846. Delegates were present from the institutions of sixteen States, namely, Vermont, New Hampshire, Massachusetts, Rhode Island, Connecticut, New York, New Jersey, Pennsylvania, Delaware, Maryland, Virginia, Georgia, Mississippi, Indiana, Illinois, and Tennessee. The convention was organized by the election of the following officers: Prof. Jonathan Knight, of New Haven, president; John Bell, M. D., of Philadelphia, and Edward Delafield, M. D., of New York, vice-presidents; and Richard D. Arnold, M. D., of Savannah, and Alfred Stillé, M.D., of Philadelphia, secretaries. The sessions of the convention were continued three days, during which all the great questions pertaining to the interests of the profession were discussed with commendable order and liberality, and resulted in the appointment of committees on the following subjects: the standard of preliminary or general education necessary to qualify individuals to enter upon the study of medicine; the standard of medical education requisite for graduation; a nomenclature of diseases; a code of ethical rules; and a plan of organization for a permanent national association. All these committees were to report in full at an adjourned meeting to be held in Philadelphia on the first Tuesday in May, 1847.

On the reassembling of the convention at the appointed time in Philadelphia, about two hundred and fifty delegates took their seats, representing forty medical societies, State and local, and twenty-eight medical colleges, embracing the institutions of twenty-two States and those of the District of Columbia. All the committees appointed at the previous meeting made able and interesting reports, which can be found in full

---

* See History of the American Medical Association, pp. 19, 20, by N. S. Davis, M. D., published by Lippincott, Grambo & Co., Philadelphia, 1855.

† For more full details in reference to this whole subject, see History of Medical Education, etc., by N. S. Davis, M. D., chapter iii, 1850.

in the first volume of Transactions of the American Medical Association. The committee on permanent organization reported a constitution and by-laws, which were adopted, and the convention was resolved into the American Medical Association, which immediately elected the following officers: President, Nathaniel Chapman, M. D., of Pennsylvania; vice-presidents, Jonathan Knight, M. D., of Connecticut, Alexander H. Stevens, M. D., of New York, James Moultrie, M.D., of South Carolina, and A. H. Buchanan, M. D., of Tennessee; secretaries, Alfred Stillé, M.D., of Philadelphia, and J. R. W. Dunbar, M. D., of Baltimore; treasurer, Isaac Hays, M. D., of Philadelphia. The association, as thus organized, adopted the code of ethics which has since become the universal law of the profession in this country, passed resolutions strongly recommending a standard of preparatory education for students before entering upon medical studies, longer annual lecture terms in the colleges, and a higher standard of medical attainments for the degree of doctor of medicine. The constitution adopted made the association essentially a representative body, composed of delegates from medical societies—State, district, and local—medical colleges, and permanent hospitals throughout the whole country. Its meetings have been held annually, and, as the constitution prohibited the holding of two consecutive meetings in the same city, they have visited successively all the larger cities of the United States, stimulating by their presence the formation of State and local societies, and bringing into closer relations, better acquaintance, and greater harmony the profession of the whole country. That the formation of the national organization gave a new impulse to professional organizations in all the States is clearly evident from the fact that, owing to causes already explained, for ten or twelve years prior to such organization medical societies had not only ceased to be formed in new localities, but many of those previously exis'ing under special charters were maintaining only a nominal existence; while at the present time we know of but one State in the Union that has not a State medical society as well as many affiliated local societies. The American Medical Association and nearly all of the more recently formed State and local societies are purely voluntary organizations, untrammelled by legal enactments or charters, but all adopting and being governed by a common code of ethics, and animated by common purposes, namely, the mutual improvement of all the members and the advancement of the interests and usefulness of the profession. When it is remembered that most of the city societies hold meetings once a month, the county and district societies from two to four times a year, and the State and national organizations annually, and that, at all these meetings, cases are reported, papers read, and views interchanged freely upon all subjects connected with the science and art of medicine, and that the national association and nearly all the State societies publish all the more important contributions of their members in annual volumes of transactions, it will be generally conceded that the aggregate value of the influence of these social organizations on the

education and usefulness of the profession cannot be easily overesti-
mated. The value of these organizations is not restricted to the profession itself, or to its indirect influence on the community by increasing
the learning and skill of their members, but to their direct influence can
be traced a very large part of all the more important sanitary measures
by which the health of cities, towns, and even whole districts of country
has been so much improved in modern times. The establishment of municipal and State boards of health, for the special protection of the people
against contagious and epidemic diseases and the preservation of vital
statistics, is preëminently due to the influence of our medical societies.

We cannot close this brief chapter on the history of our medical society
organizations better than by quoting the following from the first page
of the History of the American Medical Association, pub ished in 1855 :

It has been said by some one that associated action constitutes the mainspring, the
controlling motive power, of modern society ; and whoever surveys with the eye of
intelligence the present aspect and tendencies of civilization, will readily acknowledge
the truth of the remark. It is by the association of capital that those great enter-
prises for facilitating commerce and intercourse among States and nations are being
prosecuted with an energy and success which promise to break through the strongest
barriers of nature, and make neighbors of nations on the opposite sides of our globe.
It is by the association of mind with mind, in the church, the conference, the presby-
tery, the diocese, and the general convocations, that the moral force of Christendom is
stirred up, concentrated, and brought to act with mighty power in disseminating the
sublime truths of the Christian religion. So, too, by the association of mind with mind,
in the rapidly recurring anniversary meetings of the learned, not only is thought made
to elicit thought, and the generous ambition of one made to kindle a kindred impulse
in another, but the rich and varied fruits of many intellects are brought to a common
storehouse, and made the common property of all; for intellectual treasures, unlike
those of a material nature, neither become monopolized by concentration, lost by use,
nor diminished by diffusion or communication to others. If it is true that associated
action constitutes so prominent an element in the progressive tendencies of modern
society as a whole, it is no less so in reference to the several classes of which the whole
is composed; and of these individual classes none holds a more important or influential
relation to all the rest than that which is made up of the active practitioners of the
healing art. Forced by the nature of their calling to become preëminently cultiva-
tors of the whole field of natural science and philosophy, while they have the freest
possible access to the homes and hearts of all classes, they are daily exerting an influence over the physical and intellectual elements of society second to that of no
other class in Christendom. Hence, whatever is calculated materially to influence the
character of the medical profession is worthy of one page, at least, in the historical
records of our race.*

See History of American Medical Association, by N. S. Davis, M. D., pp. 17, 18.
Lippincott, Grambo & Co., Philadelphia, 1855.